TRANSYLVANIA STATION

The Perpetrators

Mohonk Mysteries

High Jinx
Transylvania Station
The Hood House Heist
Double Crossing
Way Out, West
The Maltese Herring

TRANSYLVANIA STATION

STATION

—

Donald & Abby
Westlake

Cover by Gahan Wilson;
back cover by Joe Servello

FIRST EDITION
Published December 1987

Dennis McMillan Publications
1995 Calais Dr. No. 3
Miami Beach, FL 33141

Distributed by Creative Arts Book Co.
833 Bancroft Way
Berkeley, CA 94710

Acknowledgements

We wish to thank the many people whose wit and work made it possible for us to stand up here as though we'd done the whole thing ourselves.

First, to Dilys Winn and Carol Brener, who thought it up and ironed the bugs out and turned it over to us as a wonderful surprise package.

And to our speakers and suspects, all of whom have taken this friviolity just seriously enough to make it work.

And then, at Mohonk Mountain House, pre-eminently to Faire Hart, who runs the program for the hotel and saves our lives at least once a day, without ever losing her optimism.

And to Barbara Seaman and Carol Schimmer, also of Mohonk, who ignore both the clock and good sense and just get the job done.

And to Annie O'Neill, graphics designer *par excellence,* who gives each Weekend its distinctive look.

And to Matthew Seaman, a skilled and imaginative cameraman/photographer/director, who every year takes our rough notes for Thursday night's narration and turns them into smooth and evocative visuals, whether film or slides.

And to the cheerful and high-spirited employees of Mohonk, who in their time have been, at our request, everything from cowboys to Transylvanian villagers.

Thank you!

The Business

The Mohonk Mysteries are the property of Donald E. and Abby Westlake and Mohonk Mountain House. They may not be presented or performed for profit.

For permission for a non-profit organization to present or perform a Mohonk Mystery, write to the publisher on your organization's letterhead.

Photos herein, unless otherwise identified, are the work of Matthew Seaman, and are the property of Matthew Seaman and Mohonk Mountain House.

Foreword

In January of 1977, two ingenious women named Dilys Winn and Carol Brener put on, at a huge and magnificently rustic mountaintop hotel ninety miles north of New York City, the world's first mystery weekend, in which the guests were invited to observe and then solve a murder. Celebrity speakers that first year included Isaac Asimov and Phyllis Whitney, and the idea was so successful it became an annual affair, and has bred imitators by now from California to the British Isles.

We'd heard of the Mohonk Mystery Weekends, but had never seen one in action until Dilys, by then running the program herself, invited us to observe the sixth in the series, *The Teacup Caper,* featuring Ruth Rendell and Frederick "Dial M for Murder" Knott. When it was over, she told us she was running out of steam and felt she needed someone else to take over. Would we? We would.

The Weekend by then had been moved to March, and was the most popular annual event at Mohonk Mountain House. The first Thursday of each December, the hotel switchboard would be opened at nine A.M. to accept Mystery reservations for the following March. Before noon on that day, the Weekend would be filled (that's more than three hundred people), with a one hundred name waiting list. The competition is so intense that there have been as many as fifty people staying at Mohonk on the Wednesday night before that reservation Thursday, simply to be at the desk the next morning to be sure of a place.

Reacting to that pressure, our third year in charge we doubled to two consecutive Mystery Weekends, with the same suspects and speakers but with the story slightly changed the second time around. And there's *still* a waiting list every December, on reservation day.

We've made some other changes, too. We still sort the guests (shall we call them *quests?* Yes) into competing teams, but we've started giving two first-place prizes. We feel there are two separate impulses at work among the quests; there are those who want to *solve the puzzle,* want to walk in the footsteps of Sherlock Holmes and Nero Wolfe; and there are those who want to take the story elements we offer and *run amok,* playing off the conventions just as much as we do. To give opportunity to both motives, we offer one team a prize for the most accurate solution and one for the most creative. And it is amazing just how much manic creativity you can unleash from three hundred bright happy people isolated for a weekend on a mountaintop.

Another change we've made is in the prizes themselves. The glory of winning has always been and still is the main award, and we still give token physical prizes as well, but we've added a prize the people really seem to like: The members of the two winning teams get to jump next year's line. If they want to come back—and most do—they have a guaranteed reservation. At our most recent Weekend, a man on a losing team was heard to say, when the winners were announced, "Damn! Back to dialing."

* * *

What is this Mystery Weekend, that people love it so? Let us describe it, step by step; not the same as being there, but just to give the idea.

The Weekend begins on Thursday, which in terms of weekends is already a plus. The quests arrive in mid-afternoon, and after dinner they meet the mystery, in the form either of a slide show or a film, with accompanying narration. Here they see the murder victim's last day, the people he/she meets, the locations, the period, the *style*.

The murder victim's last day will include encounters with ten to twelve other people, the suspects in the story. For two hours on Friday, one in the morning and one in the afternoon, these suspects are available for interrogation. The rule of the game is that the suspects *must always* tell the truth, except that the murderer will lie about the murder. (Not about motive; even the murderer will tell the truth about that. The physical facts of the murder is the only area of lies.) On the other hand, the suspects will not volunteer information; the quests have to figure out which are the right questions to ask.

On Friday night, or some time on Saturday, there's usually some other event that moves the story along. Sometime's it's a second murder, sometimes something else. (In *Transylvania Station,* Madame Openskya graciously consented to conduct a seance, during which the murder victim appeared, making that the only Weekend so far in which the quests could interrogate the victim.) And finally, on Sunday morning, the teams are asked to present their solutions, and the more elaborate the presentation, the better.

That's the bare bones of the program, but there are other diversions along the way. We always have four or five speakers to talk on subjects connected with the theme of that Weekend. These have ranged from Will Shortz, senior editor of *Games* magazine, who spoke on puzzle-solving, through cartoonist Gahan Wilson and British newspaper columnist Katharine Whitehorn, to John and Mary Maxtone-Graham, he the author of the definitive history of the trans-Atlantic passenger liners, *The Only Way to Cross,* who spoke during our ocean-voyage mystery, *Double Crossing.*

Of course, mystery and thriller writers have been prominent among our suspect/speakers. In our first five years, these included Robert Byrne, Max Allan Collins, Brian Garfield, Joe Gores, Stephen King, Peter Lovesey, Gavin Lyall, David Morrell, Edward A. Pollitz, Jr., Justin Scott, Martin Cruz Smith and Peter Straub. And on the real-life side of crime and detection, Marie Castoire told us how it felt to be a female homicide detective in Manhattan, and her husband, Mike Gatto, also a New York cop, told us some of *his* experiences.

From the beginning, Edward Gorey has set the mood by doing the theme drawing for every Weekend's brochure. And film scholar Chris Steinbrunner chooses appropriate movies to be run every night of the Weekend, with commentary by himself.

Although a few professional actors have been suspects, our usual approach is to use amateurs. (The actors were there as friends, not as pros.) Abby has been a suspect, though Don has not. Our guest speakers are always dragooned into being suspects, and we've used our friends and family as well, plus a number of employees of the hotel. We *want* the teams to feel they can put on as good a show as we can; a lot of the time, they put on a better one.

* * *

The preparation of a Mystery Weekend is unlike any other kind of storytelling we can think of, but it's storytelling. What makes it different is that it's a story told in fits and starts, by misdirection and repetition, and with such a lushness of narrative— and profusion of red herrings (and red hearings)— that the same story can be twisted into two separate solutions on the two consecutive weekends. And the way we put this story together is probably as unusual as the form itself.

First we determine the germ of an idea, a sense of what our story will be. Armed with that, we shoot our film or slides and write the accompanying narration. Then we write our suspect biographies, telling each suspect, "This is who you are and this is what you know." The suspects are not told the whole story, only their part in it, which means the suspects get some surprises, too, during the interrogations. And finally we write the full story of the mystery, the Truth.

This piecemeal creation is echoed in the piecemeal unleashing of the story during the Mystery Weekend, beginning with the narrated film or slides, the interrogations, whatever other event we've thrown in to keep the story moving, and culminating on Sunday morning, when the teams of quests tell their versions of the story back to us in their own way, with singing and dancing and bad puns and little playlets and costumes and signs and props and general hilarity. After which, to close the Weekend, we tell them the Truth.

This book is a recreation of such a Mohonk Mystery Weekend, or as close as we can come to the real thing on the printed page. The book is divided into four sections, approximating the experience of the Weekend:

1. The Narration. This is the narration Don gives on Thursday evening, accompanying the film or slides.

2. The Suspect Biographies. This, in a slightly modified form, is what each suspect is given before the Weekend. Some repetition here is inevitable, because at least two people will know virtually every fact or event in the story.

3. The Quiz. We don't have this quiz at the Weekend itself, because the quests are interacting with the suspects and the events, and are presenting their solutions in their own way. We tried to think of an equivalent to those presentations, and this is it. Abby has done a number of magazine quizzes, so she's adapted that form and our story-form and fitted them together.

4. The Truth. This, again in a slightly modified form, is what we tell the quests at the end of the Weekend.

The Mohonk Mystery Weekends did not begin as stories to be read, but as stories to be told and retold and searched for and adapted from and played with like Silly Putty. The idea of it is *story* as *game*. We hope we've made the transition successfully to a more or less normal narrative, but it needn't end there. It's still a game, and you're invited to play.

Happy solving!

The Strange Case
of the
Westlake Stationery
by Stephen King

I suppose you'd think Don Westlake's stationery was only bizarre if you'd never read his novels and stories. If you have, you understand. If you understand, it becomes pretty funny. Not as funny as the man himself—when he's in the mood, Donald Westlake can be downright hilarious—but pretty funny.

Which might seem odd, at least on the surface.

After all, Westlake is a writer who has spent most of his career fascinated by criminals and capers. If that was all, I guess he'd be a pretty ordinary sort of genre writer. But he is also a keen observer of human nature, and no one is more appreciative of the peaks of foolishness to which we mortals can and do aspire. A critic could say Westlake has evolved through three distinct stages, each illustrated by a fictional crook.

First there was Parker. When it comes to that quality Ian Fleming referred to once as sensayuma (as in "he's a guy wit no sensayuma"), Parker and stone plinths run about neck and neck. In *Butcher's Moon,* the last novel Westlake wrote about him, one of Parker's antagonists presents Parker with the severed finger of a colleague (you can't say "friend"; Parker has none, with the possible exception of Handy McKay, whose diner in Presque Isle serves the best hash-and-eggs in the State . . . and, since I've lived in Maine all my life, I should know). Parker pulls a gun and aims it at the man who has, you should pardon the expression, just given him the finger.

"No!" the horrified fellow cries. "I'm just the messenger!"

"Now you're the message," Parker deadpans, and blows him away. This is as close as Parker ever comes to humor, I believe.

This man, who is described in Westlake's (writing as Richard Stark) first novel about him as "having a face that looked hacked from an oak tree," survived botched jobs, double-crossing partners, even the Organization (whatever *that* is). Ironically, the only assassin he couldn't evade was Westlake's own sense of humor. Westlake had apparently passed the point where he could view Parker seriously. More ironically, the second stage of Westlake's criminal development (and he *is* a habitual offender, friends, make no mistake about *that)* is represented by the very man who suffered the fingerectomy (digitectomy?). This gentleman, Alan Grofield by name, is a proficient thief with a sense of humor. An actor who is a spinoff of the Parker books, Grofield pulls scores to keep his little theater in business. He is his own artistic grants-in-aid director, you might say. And whether he's in hot water or a hot woman, he always hears the appropriate movie soundtrack music in his head.

From the cocoon which is Grofield finally comes the ultimate Westlake creation: a dazed butterfly which spreads its magnificent wings, dries them, flutters them preparatory to its maiden flight . . . which ends with a direct hit on the nearest tree. I am speaking, of course, about that literary equivalent of Murph the Surf, Dortmunder. Parker is an expert thief with no sense of humor; Grofield is an expert thief who does have one; Dortmunder doesn't have much sense of humor, but he's so goddam inept you can die laughing while he bumbles his way through capers like Charlie Chaplin bumbling his way through *Modern Times*. Could Dortmunder steal candy from a baby? The answer is simple: of course not. He would reach for the candy, the carriage would start to roll, the baby would bite Dortmunder in that excruciatingly sensitive web of flesh between thumb and first finger, and Dortmunder would end up getting busted not for candy-theft but kidnaping.

What does all this have to do with Donald Westlake's stationery?

Well, he steals it, you see.

If you consider taking a little hotel stationery *stealing,* that is. It's not the same as taking the towels, of course; I mean, it's there for the guests, but . . . well . . . the fact is, he seems to have an *awful* lot of it. One is led to the inescapable conclusion that as Westlake and his charming wife Abby travel about, from the redwood forests to the New York highlands, from the sparkling deserts to the gulfstream waters, he finds hotel and motel stationery made for him . . . . . and him.

When you receive a letter on Holiday Inn stationery asking if you'd care to spend two weekends in upstate New York playing a Wolfman sort of character in a mystery Westlake himself has created, it is very difficult to say no. And Donald Westlake has his own peculiar but effective methods of persuasion. "When I agree to things this far in advance," he wrote (his letter came to me a year or so before the two

Transylvania Station weekends), "I usually agree on three assumptions: that somehow the time to actually *do* something that far in the future will never come; even if it does, the Big One will probably start between my acceptance and the time when I actually have to fulfill my obligation; and even if the Big One *doesn't* start between then and now, I'll probably die."

How can one resist such logic, especially when it 1.) offers not one but two "comped" weekends at the Mohonk Mountain House, one of the oddest, oldest, and most beautiful resort hotels in America, not just for me but for my wife and kids; 2.) offers a chance for me to ham it up outrageously as a kind of full-moon Jordy Verrill; and, of course, 3.) comes on Holiday Inn stationery.

I accepted.

Of course.

Westlake, a gentleman to the core, crazed sense of humor notwithstanding, immediately dropped me a thank-you note.

On stationery with a letterhead from a Sheraton in Kansas City.

Does he *file* the stuff, I sometimes wonder? Does he maybe *alphabetize* it? O, bootless queries! Might as well ask who trims the barber's beard in a town that can only support one pro (the answer, of course, is that she's never had to worry about it—just so you won't stay awake all night wondering, y' know).

The mystery weekends which Don and Abby Westlake run are built on "themes," and their teamwork is as good as his ability to tempt writers such as myself who seem to "fit" that year's theme to come and join in. Part of the attraction is a chance to hobnob with old pals like Peter Straub and Gahan Wilson

(Peter, with a little white-face, turned into a suitably urbane vampire, and Gahan positively outdid himself as The Mad Doctor Who Turns Out To Be A Charlatan); part of it is the chance to meet and talk with writers one has admired but never met (other than Donald himself, who I had met, but under those crazy circumstances which accompany book-signings—at such times, you can barely *think* coherently, let alone hold a conversation—my largest charge was meeting Justin Scott, whose work I admire immensely, from *The Turning* to *The Shipkiller* to last year's *Rampage);* and part of it is the eternal lure of the mystery itself.

I'll not describe the creation or presentation of that mystery, nor will I go into the formation of the teams (i.e., paying guests) that compete in solving, or the judging . . . although, on the latter subject, I might mention that Westlake was less than consoling. He told us the competition was always fierce, and added: "We make it a policy to always keep a couple of stationwagons idling outside while the winners are announced. Just keep that in mind . . . and notice the nearest exit is forty feet to the left of the judges' table. In the event of an, uh, event, Peter [Straub] would hold the door for the ladies. You, Steve, would be last. You're the biggest, so you'd be in charge of blocking."

Just like Parker, scoping out all possible contingencies.

I cast an anxious eye at the teams as they filed in for the Final Judgement. Yes, they looked serious, all right, outrageous costumes or not. *Deadly* serious. I asked Don if he thought any of these people might carry knives. Or, uh, you know, things that go bang and fire projectiles at a high speed.

Don offered me a quiet sn..ie and asked if I had a business manager.

Mystified, I tol.. nim I did.

"Is he any good?" Don asked.

I said he was very good, feeling that I had somehow stumbled into a bizarre E.F. Hutton ad, and all these people filing into the central meeting hall at the Mountain Lodge would in a moment or two fall silent, turning toward us with hands cupped at ears.

"If he's good, you won't die intestate," Don said with that same dreamy, comforting smile, "and I'm sure Tabby would make a wonderful literary executor."

I'm convinced the guy really *is* one of the finest humorists working in American letters today (anyone who can describe that great humanitarian Idi Amin, as Westlake did in *Kahawa,* as resembling "a large, overripe black olive" gets *my* vote), but sometimes he can be every bit as funny as a screen door in a submarine.

Well, I got through the weekend . . . got through *both* of them, in fact, and I understand why people come back again and again; why a yearly event which was at first undersubscribed now has to turn away applicants. Westlake is a wonderful host and master of ceremonies; the paying customers make the mostly well-mannered World Fantasy Convention attendees look like boors (and the attendees of your average SF con like chittering, bad-tempered monkeys). Although the weekends had their absurd moments (here is King with fake hair glued all over his hands and face, sitting inside a set constructed to look like a 17th century jail-cell in the Bastille, typing away on a word processor for no reason King can quite discern while people outside file past with the curiosity usually reserved for the two-headed cow in the carnival), the ambiance of the Mountain House (which, during the first weekend, was actually cut off from neighboring New Paltz briefly by waters flooding over lowland roads . . . I kept thinking of *Ten Little Indians* and about how much Donald Westlake resembled my conception of Mr. Justice Wargrave) and the amiability of the participants made it a cheerful and memorable event.

Now comes this book from the estimable Mr. Dennis McMillan.

Dennis sent me a check for a hundred bucks.

Dennis, I'll send it back if the Westlake manuscript comes on hotel stationery . . . and if you send me a Xerox.

I've never been in Don and Abby's house.

The wallpaper . . . the *toilet* paper . . . I wonder . . .

Could it be that . . . ?

No, surely not. But . . . maybe . . .

Day's Inn?

Caesar's Palace?

Best Western?

Or maybe . . .

The Speakers

Andrew Benepe, monster maker, whose creations have lumbered and slithered through any number of movies as well as the off-Broadway production of *Little Shop of Horrors* and the theme disco *Area*.

Stephen King, co-author of *The Talisman*.

Peter Straub, co-author of *The Talisman*.

Gahan Wilson, cartoonist and writer, regularly in *The New Yorker* and *Playboy*.

The Cast

Count Alucard, Peter Straub
Eeyore, David Duffield
Dr. Rollo Frankenfield, Gahan Wilson
Joseph Gawker, Byrne Fone
Lily Languish, Dorenna Hart
Mrs. Morbidd, Eve Bookey
Brick Newborn, Chet Davis
Giddy Newborn, Kate Coler
Madame Openskya, Gloria Hoye
Primeva, Kate Duffield
Barry Talmud, Stephen King
Clara Whiteworthy, Susan Lohmann

Here's Joseph Gawker, librarian by trade.

A silently waiting and covered black coach.

The Narration

East of the Moldau, far east of the Rhine,
Stands Transylvania Station, the end of the line.

No one gets off there, no, no one who knows,
The local recitals of terror and woes.

Yet here's Joseph Gawker, librarian by trade,
Arrived on the local and quite unafraid,

Hired and paid a quite goodly amount
To sort the library of the neighborhood count.

Watch him, with some trepidation, approach
A silently waiting and covered black coach.

The coach door swings open, sans driver or groom,
And Joseph then enters the Stygian gloom.

At once the coach hastens, it's seeming to fly,
While from hiding the townsfolk all watch it go by.

Pounded and jolted and taken aback,
Joseph stares out at a forest deep black.

While beyond that bleak landscape, both blasted and
    charred,
Rises the castle of Count Alucard.

The air is perfumed with a mildewy musk.

Straight to the gate those two horses do roar,
Into the courtyard, and stop at the door.

Which opens and then, with no further ado,
A bustling and fidgety woman steps through.

Mrs. Jane Morbidd she says is her name,
The keeping of Alucard's house is her game.

Through the doorway she leads him, and into the
    hall,
Where shadows mysterious veil every wall.

Where the air is perfumed with a mildewy musk,
And the housekeeper says, "The Count rises at dusk.

"For now, you must want to refresh, I assume,
So pick up your bag, and I'll show you your room."

It surely must seem then, as Joseph complies,
All around in the darkness are close watching eyes.

Up the staircase they climb, as she says, with a frown,
"It's the new railroad tunnel that's brought you to
    town."

"Oh, no," Joseph answers, "I'm no engineer.
The sorting of books is the reason I'm here."

An odd-looking woman in gypsy costume.

He'll never escape from Madame Openskya.

"The books!" Morbidd cries, and her teeth seem to
    grind.
"If you poke round in there, then who knows what
    you'll find.

"But here is your room." And she gives him side looks,
Saying, "*I* wouldn't want to be buried in books."

Alone in his room, Joseph studies the place,
And is happy to find it a quite pleasant space.

Unpacking, he opens the roomy armoire,
And discovers a person he thinks quite bizarre.

An odd-looking woman in gypsy costume,
Who says, "I am sorry, I'm in the wrong room."

"Just what are you doing here?" Joseph demands,
And takes some thick documents out of her hands.

She snatches them back: "These won't be for you.
Barry Talmud's the man I'll be giving these to.

"He's a fugitive here in this land, a pariah,
But he'll never escape from Madame Openskya."

With which she departs, leaving Joseph in doubt,
And to wonder what that scene had been all about.

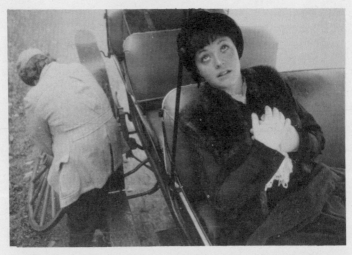

He finds himself now in the most dire straits.

Let us make haste now, it cannot be far.

While far and away, far out over the moor,
Brick Newborn has taken an unwise detour.

A writer of thrillers back home in the States,
He finds himself now in the most dire straits.

With his new bride, young Giddy, who may have just
    swooned,
He's stuck in this forest, he's stranded, marooned.

The coach wheel is broken, the horses distressed,
Poor Brick doesn't know which next move would be
best.

"Look, Giddy! Just gaze upon yon rising spire.
Surely we'll find there both comfort and fire.

"Fine dinner, a pillow to rest your sweet head,
Some wise conversation, and then off to bed."

Giddy's delighted, she knew her man could
Somehow remove them both out of this wood.

"Oh, yes, Brick, let's hurry, how brilliant you are.
Let us make haste now, it cannot be far."

There's nothing to see in the wall looking-glass.

While sundown approaches, our Joseph unpacks,
Then dresses for dinner. It's time to relax.

But he's startled, while trying to tie his cravat,
By a thing at the window— Is it a bat?

There's nothing to see in the wall looking-glass.
What could it have been? Oh, well, well, let it pass.

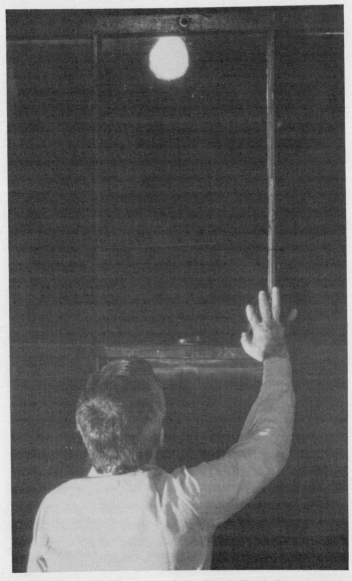

She knows I'll remember the full of the moon.

Leaving the room, he goes out to the stair,
And finds an odd person is lurking out there.

The man seems both gloomy and greatly depressed,
And dinner seems not that for which he has dressed.

"You're new here," he cries, when he sees Joseph's
    face,
And Joseph explains then his role in the case.

"Barry Talmud's my name," says the woebegone gent.
"Why, then," Joseph cries, "that was no accident.

"A Romany woman I found stowed away,
Had messages for you, or so she did say.

"She told me her name, it was Madame Open—"
"No, no!" Talmud cries, "say it's not her again!"

He stares out the window, intoning, "So soon?
She knows I'll remember the full of the moon."

With that he turns round, and he looks very grave.
And he says, "I believe I will now go and shave."

Joseph, unknowing, descends to his fate.

Down in the parlor, the guests all await,
As Joseph, unknowing, descends to his fate.

Arriving downstairs, Joseph finds in the hall
A person waiting, imposing and tall.

He takes Joseph's hand, and his grip is quite hard.
"You are welcome," he says. "I am Count Alucard.

"Come into my parlor." And Joseph obeys.
And enters a room where the fires do blaze.

Where women and men all quite gracefully dressed
Turn about quite politely to greet this new guest.

The count says, "Here's new blood has joined us
     today.
Young Joseph Gawker has come here to stay.

You must warm yourself quickly.

She is frail and pathetic and really quite ill.

"Now, this is my daughter, Primeva. My dear,
The gentleman we've been expecting is here."

Joseph, to greet, takes her hand in his own,
Is startled to find it as cold as a stone.

"You are chilled," he says. "Do, please, I wish to
    exhort,
You must warm yourself quickly with claret or port."

"Thank you," she answers, "but I'm feeling fine.
And as it so happens, I never drink . . . wine."

And here's Lily Languish, the next introduced.
Her cheeks are so pallid, her hair quite unloosed.

The ward of the count, by her dead father's will,
She is frail and pathetic and really quite ill.

But here is her doctor, who's called Frankenfield,
Who most worriedly says, "I had hoped she'd be
    healed.

"But I just have not yet found the right antidote.
Nor do I fathom those scars on her throat."

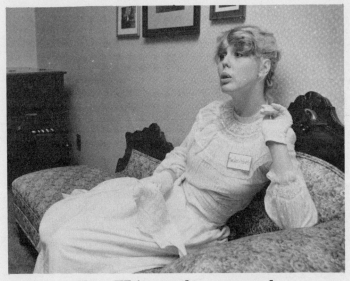

Clara Whiteworthy on a couch

Now Frankenfield turns and says, "Clara, come here.
I wish you to meet Joseph Gawker, my dear.

"Miss Whiteworthy here, I am happy to say,
Has recently joined me as my fiancée."

"Are you a scientist?" Clara then asks.
"No, a librarian. Much simpler tasks."

Interrupted just then by a man at the door,
Frankenfield says, "My assistant, Eeyore."

To the doctor the servant a nervous wave gives,
Crying "Come to the lab with me, Master. It lives!"

"Rollo, not now," his fiancée entreats,
But Frankenfield answers, "I must go, my sweets."

"Just remember," she cautions, "I did tell you so.
There are things here below man was not meant to
    know."

And yet I've this feeling I've been here before.

To sup at the table while absent the host.

As Frankenfield leaves, with Eeyore at his side,
Mrs. Morbidd appears, with Brick Newborn and
bride.

"Their coach has broke down, Count, can they stay
the night?"
"Oh, my," Giddy cries. "I've had just such a fright!"

"It's our first time," Brick says, "that we've been to
this shore,
And yet I've this feeling I've been here before."

"You are welcome," the count says, "to all that is
mine.
And now please excuse me. I'll pray while you dine."

With which, just as though she weighed nothing at
all,
He takes Lily up, bears her out to the hall.

Up the stairs they depart, with no further goodbye,
In their wake leaving only Miss Lily's faint sigh.

Primeva behind them, the darkness ahead,
They leave while the guests gather round to be fed.

Of all the strange episodes, this was the most,
To sup at the table while absent the host.

Later, quite restless, and pacing his room,
Joseph feels dankness, the chill of the tomb.

Knowing no reason to wait until light,
He chooses to see the library tonight.

For most of the night, he is there to explore
Many a quaint and curious volume of forgotten lore.

Are others observing him, all unbeknown?
Or is our friend Joseph now all, all alone?

When dawn comes, the books are deserted once more,
While up in his room, Joseph lies on the floor.

Can something be not right about Joseph's bed?
No. Something's not right about Joseph. He's dead.

And you will soon find there, if you chance to check,
Two tiny new wounds in the side of his neck.

Is the killer of Gawker the Count, Alucard?
Or his daughter, Primeva? Or Lily, the ward?

Was the gypsy the killer? Or the man she pursues?
Or is Mrs. Morbidd the one to accuse?

Could Brick or his Giddy have put him to death?
Could Eeyore have helped him to breathe his last
breath?

Could the Doctor or Clara have been so barbarian
As to put the quietus to this poor librarian?

You'll all have a long time for examination
Before your departure from Transylvania Station.

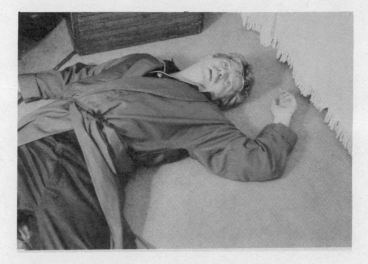

Standing (l to r): Madame Openskya, Count Alucard, Dr. Frankenfield, Clara Whiteworthy, Primeva, Giddy Newborn, Brick Newborn, Mrs. Morbidd. Crouching and seated (l to r): Eeyore, Lily Languish, Barry Talmud.

Biographies

Mrs. Morbidd

Welcome to Castle Alucard. Make yourselves comfortable, if you can. I'm the housekeeper here; Mrs. Morbidd's the name, born in New York City, USA. There never was a Mr. Morbidd, me not being the kind that likes to be tied down, but the title comes in handy.

How did I get from Hell's Kitchen to Transylvania? It's a long story. Let's just say that a few years ago it seemed like a good idea to get out of town for awhile. Me and some of my associates were involved in a lucrative racket involving the sale of stocks, many of which were worth less than the paper they were written on. Everything was going fine and then a customer caught wise and one of my associates took it upon himself to silence the fellow permanently. Well, between my trigger-happy associates and the nosy New York City police, I didn't see much of a future for myself. I skipped.

I left New York on the first ship going out, signing on as a cook. When the ship landed in Bremerhaven I got on a train. I took that train as far as it went, and then I took the next train and the next, and wound up at Transylvania Station, the end of the line. I asked around for work and found out that the count up here at Castle Alucard was looking for a housekeeper who spoke English. That was three years ago and I've been here since.

The work itself isn't too tough. Housework is not what you'd call my *forte,* but no one here gives me a hard time about the cobwebs and the dust pussies, and if they don't like my cooking they don't complain.

Most of them don't even eat. Count Alucard and his daughter, Primeva, both have some disease and lately the doctor's been feeding them sheepfat, to try to cure them. It just makes two less mouths for me to feed. And the count's ward, Lily Languish, is too sick to eat much of anything. So that leaves me five people to cook for—Dr. Frankenfield,, Clara Whiteworthy, Eeyore, me, and just for the past few days, Barry Talmud. (That's up until yesterday when the others arrived—I'll get around to *them* later.)

Here's something that puzzles me; every night someone, I don't know who, steals food out of the kitchen. It's been going on as long as I've been here.

That's not the only strange thing around here. This castle contains the weirdest collection of oddballs and fruitcakes this side of the circus. Count Alucard and Primeva have this hideous disease. The count's a nice enough gent but Primeva's a real witch. I'd be afraid to cross her. And Lily's a vampire if you ask me. She's got those two little marks on her neck, everyone knows what *they* mean. I keep myself protected, with bunches of garlic at my window, and I always wear a cross under my dress, even though I'm not a churchgoer. Then there's Eeyore, the handicapped handyman, with his horrible scarred face, mumbling and spitting and twitching. Sometimes he turns himself into a bat and creeps about on the outside walls of the castle. I've seen it with my own eyes, honest!

Lately I've been wearing wolfbane too, because of

Barry Talmud. When he first turned up here two years ago he seemed like a nice young fellow. He's a railway engineer, working on that big tunnel they're building. The count's a big cheese in the Transylvania Transit Authority, so Barry stayed here—also because the count and Primeva both fancied him as son-in-law material. This would have been a good deal for Barry, being as the count is filthy rich and Primeva is his only heir, but nothing came of it. Barry went off and married this gypsy fortune-teller, Maria Openskya.

Here's a weird coincidence—three years ago, just before I got into all that trouble back in New York, I went to a tearoom on Fifth Avenue to have my future looked into. The woman who read the tea leaves was this very same gypsy, Madame Openskya! She predicted trouble ahead for me, and was she ever right. That's how I know she has Powers, so when she turned up here I made sure to stay on her good side. Two months ago Barry and Maria split up and Maria started using her Powers to turn Barry into a werewolf. He keeps getting hairier—clumps of shaggy brown wolf hair all over his body and face. He disappeared for a while and nobody knew where he was, but two days ago Primeva told me he was hiding *here* in the castle. She asked me to bring him a dinner tray—she and the count have been looking after him, hiding him from Maria.

I went straight to Maria and told her. (She lives in the gypsy camp, at the bottom of the mountain.) Maria gave me wolfbane to protect myself, and told me that as long as the hair wasn't growing on the palms of his hands Barry wasn't yet a werewolf and I would be safe. When I brought him the tray I checked, and it was all right. Even so, I put the tray down and got out of there fast, let me tell you!

Compared with all these weirdo Transylvanians, Doctor Frankenfield and Clara Whiteworthy are regular types—maybe a little on the shady side, but who am I to judge? They got here five months ago. He's supposed to be treating the Alucards for their skin disease and Lily for whatever she's got. He hasn't made any progress, which isn't surprising, considering he's no more of a doctor than I am. How do I know? It takes one con artist to know another. He's not a bad sort though. If I have to tell you everything, I'll admit that him and me have a bit of a thing going. I could see he and his so-called fiancée weren't that cozy (a housekeeper gets to know who sleeps where), so I threw him a wink, he winked back, and now I visit him on the sly at night—not every night, but often enough.

As for that little baggage who calls herself Clara Whiteworthy with her la di da manners and her phoney southern accent, I was on to her from the day she walked in. Cora Geckle is her real name, a chippie from Canarsie. She used to work in a house on the Bowery, and was one of the girls my associates and I sometimes employed to entertain visiting marks. She didn't remember me but I surely knew her! Shortly after she arrived I went up to her room and told her what I knew, and suggested she'd like to make it worth my while to keep mum. (Of course I protected myself by telling her I'd hidden an envelope containing the hard facts in a place where it would be discovered in the event of my demise—I wasn't born yesterday!) Cora—or Clara—carried on that she didn't have any money of her own, but I figured a girl like her would find a way to get cash, and she did. Thanks to her I've assembled a pretty nice nest egg, which I hope to use very soon to blow the dust of this joint off my boots and get back to New York.

Which brings us up to yesterday, and the sudden arrival and even more sudden departure of Joseph Gawker. I say sudden because, until he appeared at the door I had never heard his name, and had no idea he was expected. You'd think somebody might bother to tell me when company is coming, but no. There was a knock at the door and there stood this chap. "I'm Joseph Gawker," he said. "Count Alucard is expecting me." I introduced myself and took his bags, the heft of which led me to believe he was planning a long visit. While we walked upstairs I explained that the count was napping, and asked if he was here about the railway tunnel. He informed me that he was a librarian, here to work on the count's library.

Well, this gave me pause. Clara, formerly Cora, has been dipping into the count's library. More than once I've spied her taking dusty old tomes out of the room in a fairly secretive manner, and as I've never seen her returning any, and as I don't see her as the literary sort, it is my surmise that she sells these books, possibly on those trips she keeps making to Budapest to buy dresses. Which is fine by me, being as the money lines my pockets, but I didn't like the thought that someone else might tumble to our setup.

I decided to cross that bridge if and when I came to it, and took Mr. Gawker to one of the guest rooms, which I keep made up just in case. I left him there and went back to my duties. There was another interruption a few hours later: a young couple on their honeymoon, Brick and Giddy Newborn. They told me their coach had broken down nearby and they needed a bed for the night. I brought them upstairs to the parlor, where the count, Primeva, Lily, the doc, Clara-Cora, and Joseph Gawker had gathered before dinner. The count very generously offered them the hospitality of his castle, and I showed them their room so they could dress for dinner. Then I went back to the kitchen.

Nothing else unusual happened last night. I served dinner to the doc, Clara-Cora, Gawker and the young couple. The count, Primeva and Lily had retired earlier, as usual. As I was clearing the dishes away Joseph asked me to wake him early in the morning so he could get to work right away. I gave Eeyore his usual tray in his room in the basement. I went to bed early and alone.

In the morning I went to awaken Joseph Gawker and got the fright of my life! He was dead, lying on the floor in his dressing gown, face up with his tongue sticking out and his eyes staring and two little round marks on his neck just like Lily Languish's, and the window wide open where the vampire flew in, and the rank smell of garlic over everything and . . . I ran and got the doc and he came and after I calmed down a little bit I went and told everyone else what had happened. And now I've got all my suitcases packed and as soon as I possibly can I'm getting back on that train and going home to New York.

Brick Newborn

Hi. Brick Newborn's the name; I'm thirty years old, a native of Albany, New York, a novelist by trade. You may have seen my books. I write romantic thrillers under the name of Mrs. Henrietta Thrale, and ghost stories as Morglu Clump.

Giddy Strick is the only girl I've ever loved. She's just twenty years old, from a fine Albany family. Three weeks ago this darling girl did me the very great honor of becoming my bride. After the wedding in Albany, we sailed to Europe on the Charnelia and made our way here, to Transylvania.

It was dear Giddy's idea to come here for the honeymoon. Neither of us had ever been to Europe or anywhere. Giddy's never even been to New York, although I've been there of course, meeting with my publishers and doing research. You'd think a girl like Giddy would want to go to Paris or London for her honeymoon, but no, it had to be Transylvania. Giddy's dad, Judge Strick, had a sister, Giddy's Aunt Alexis, who married some sort of nobleman and disappeared in these parts years and years ago, before my Giddy was born. The whole Strick family is obsessed with Aunt Alexis. She was an amateur artist and the walls of the Strick home are just about papered with watercolors she sent home. I find them pretty weird—gloomy dark interiors, fantastical landscapes—more Morglu Clump than Brick Newborn.

But Giddy loves them and wanted to see the place where they were painted, so we came to Transylvania.

Creepy as the pictures were, they were nothing compared to the reality. The trouble began yesterday afternoon. We were driving through fairly rough territory—blasted heath sort of place—and, except for some frightened-looking peasants who scurried out of our path like insects, we hadn't seen a fellow human being for hours. It was wet and foggy to begin with and now evening was approaching. I wasn't at all sure we were on the right road or even a road at all, and *then* the d—d wheel broke. Poor Giddy fainted straightaway. I revived her with a drop of the brandy I'd brought along for emergencies. "Oh Brick," said my poor little bride, "what are we going to do?"

At that moment, through a gap in the clouds, I glimpsed the towers of Castle Alucard. It was a welcome sight, I can tell you. Dear Giddy put her little hand in mine and we made our way through the forest to the door of the castle, arriving just as night fell.

My persistent knocking on the door eventually resulted in it being opened by a small, not very friendly woman. Imagine my astonishment when she responded to my schoolboy German in unmistakeable New Yorkese! Her name, we learned, was Jane Morbidd and she was housekeeper to Count Alucard, proprietor of the castle in which we found ourselves. I described our predicament and she allowed as how we could stay.

"Follow me," she told us, and we did. Giddy clutched my hand as we hurried through the dank stone passages. There were cobwebs everywhere. Jane Morbidd certainly wasn't any great shakes at housekeeping, I whispered to Giddy.

I'd been bothered all day by a pesky sense of *deja vu*—the feeling that I'd been here before. When Mrs. Morbidd opened the vast oak door to the parlor I suddenly realized what it was—Castle Alucard, inside and out, was familiar to me from the pictures in Giddy's house in Albany. I cried out and would have shared my insight with Giddy but at that moment I had to step aside, to make room for two men who were leaving the room we were entering. We weren't introduced but I later learned that they were Doctor Rollo Frankenfield, an American doctor who was the count's personal physician, and his assistant, Eeyore, a hideously disfigured hunchback.

We followed Mrs. Morbidd into the parlor, a cavernous space whose chill was barely altered by a fireplace large enough to fry a mammoth. The count came forward to greet us. You've met him yourself so I needn't tell you what an odd fish he is, with his pale almost irridescent skin. But once I got used to his appearance I found him a regular chap, gracious and hospitable; a true gentleman. He made us both feel right at home. The others were an ill-assorted lot. There was the count's daughter, Primeva, just as pale and sickly as her dad, but not nearly as nice; his ward, Lily, who appeared to be near death; Dr. Frankenfield's fiancée, Clara Whiteworthy (a real looker); and Joseph Gawker, a librarian from Binghamton, New York, who was also a new arrival, here to catalog the count's books. Gawker took me aside briefly to ask if I'd ever met the doctor before, said he seemed familiar to him. Of course I hadn't.

Shortly after our arrival the count announced that he was retiring for the evening. He picked Lily Languish up out of her wheelchair, and, followed by Primeva, left the room, which, it being no later than seven P.M., I found peculiar to say the least.

Dinner was announced soon afterward. The doctor returned from wherever he'd been to join us, making five at the table: myself, Giddy, Joseph Gawker, Miss Whiteworthy and the doc. Mrs. Morbidd served us—in fact I have yet to see any other servants here.

Conversation didn't exactly sparkle over dinner. Gawker and I chatted about our travels, and I recounted the story of Giddy's long lost Aunt Alexis. I would have liked to have learned more about the Alucard family but neither the doctor nor Miss Whiteworthy was forthcoming. For an engaged couple they didn't seem especially fond of one another.

After dinner Mrs. Morbidd led Giddy and me through the labyrinthine passages of the castle to our room. We spent a restless night. I guess the excitement of the day, and also perhaps the unaccustomed richness of the cuisine, made sleep difficult. Giddy seemed troubled, but she didn't want to talk. We were both up several times.

At one point I went looking for a glass of water—which I never found—and I saw a strange woman on the stairs who, oddly enough, I think I recognized! Three years ago, in the course of researching one of the Henrietta Thrale books, I spent some time talking with a fortuneteller who worked at a gypsy tearoom in New York City. I met with her several times and she was most helpful—I can't recall her name, Madame Something. (I should make it clear that there was nothing whatsoever of a passionate nature between us—in fact, there's never been anything of that sort in my life except for my own sweet little Giddy.)

In the morning Mrs. Morbidd awoke us early to announce that Joseph Gawker had died, apparently of unnatural causes. We were both very shocked and saddened, for he seemed like a fine chap. I was worried at how Giddy would take the news but my brave girl stood up to it well.

As soon as the investigation is over I hope to take Giddy and head for Albany, New York, shaking the dust and cobwebs of Castle Alucard from our shoes forever. This whole business is far too much like a Morglu Clump story for my taste.

Giddy Newborn

My name is Giddy Newborn and I'm twenty years old. (I almost said "Giddy Strick"—I've only been married for three weeks and I'm still not used to my new name!) Brick and I are on our honeymoon.

It was my idea to come to Transylvania. Long ago, before I was born, my Aunt Alexis Strick came to this part of the world to work as a nurse. She married an important nobleman and they lived in a castle. She used to write to my dad and send drawings and watercolors she made of the place where she lived. Then she stopped writing and no one ever heard from her again, or found out what had happened to her. Daddy never got over it. I grew up hearing about Aunt Alexis, and looking at pictures of the castle where she lived, so naturally I wanted to visit Transylvania on my honeymoon. I thought it would be a beautiful romantic mysterious place. Now I think it's a hateful place, and I wish we'd stayed home and gone to Niagara Falls.

Brick probably told you all about how our carriage broke down and we had to spend the night in this moldly old castle, with all these weird people. The count and his daughter have some awful skin disease. It really gave me the creeps when he kissed my hand! Lily Languish is about my age, but we don't have much in common. The doctor and his fiancée, Clara

Whiteworthy, are Americans, like us, but they weren't the least bit friendly or welcoming. Mrs. Morbidd is another cold fish. I wouldn't give two American cents for the lot of them, not even if you threw in Castle Alucard!

Joseph Gawker seemed like a pretty nice person. I just about died when I met him because he looks almost exactly like a person I once knew, Dr. Stephen Gawker—I'm pretty sure they're brothers. I'll tell you about it but you have to *swear* that you won't tell Brick. I'd die if he found out. Cross your heart?

O.K. Daddy had corresponded with Dr. Gawker—I don't know how it began, but Stephen Gawker had lived in Transylvania and Daddy hoped he might have some clue to what had become of Aunt Alexis. Nothing came of it. Then Stephen came back to America and stopped in Albany to meet Daddy. And me. This is really embarrassing, trying to tell this story. I had just become engaged to Brick, and he was away in New York on business and I guess I was having second thoughts about settling down and getting married so young. And Stephen Gawker— he's much older, very handsome and sophisticated and suave—he just swept me off my feet! Looking back, I think he was a practiced seducer. Anyway, I ran off to Lake George with him. I spent one night with him, then, in the morning, I came to my senses and took the first train back to Albany. I never saw or heard from Stephen Gawker after that day. Thank goodness no one knows a thing about it. It was a terrible mistake and I just hope and pray my dear husband Brick never learns of it.

You can imagine how I felt when I met Joseph Gawker last night. He looked *so* much like Stephen.

And at dinner he mentioned to Dr. Frankenfield that he had a brother named Stephen who was a doctor. Would Stephen have been enough of a cad to have boasted to his brother about what happened between us? Would Joseph tell Brick? I was so upset I couldn't eat or sleep last night.

In the middle of the night I got up and left the room to look for the you-know-what (which I didn't find) and I saw Count Alucard walking down the hallway carrying a tray of food. He didn't notice me. He didn't eat dinner with us, which was pretty rude if you ask me, so maybe he got hungry for a midnight snack. Everyone in Transylvania is so odd and peculiar, I just can't *wait* to get back to Albany.

In the morning Mrs. Morbidd woke us up to announce that Joseph Gawker had been killed. It sounds awful but I was relieved to hear the news!

Barry Talmud under interrogation

Barry Talmud

Pleased to meet you—Talmud's the name. I'm an American citizen, a railway engineer by profession. I came here to Transylvania two years ago, hired by the Transylvania Transit Authority to work on the great railway tunnel through Black Mountain, which is now near completion.

When I first arrived, Count Alucard very kindly and hospitably let me stay here, at the castle. I came to know him and his daughter, Primeva, quite well. At first, as an American I didn't know how I'd feel about living in a castle with European aristocrats. Where I come from everyone's pretty much equal. But the Alucards made me feel right at home. The count's a fine cultivated man, very public-spirited. And Primeva's a fine girl, a little shy until you get to know her. They both speak excellent English—in fact, the count insists that English be spoken here at Castle Alucard.

I had been here for several months when, one night, the count confided that he hoped I might fall in love with Primeva and marry her. I was astonished. The Alucards come from a very distinguished ancient family and they are very wealthy, so it was a great honor. Nevertheless I had to tell the count, as tactfully as possible, that I was not the man for Primeva. There were two reasons for my decision.

The first is that all the Alucards suffer from a rare hereditary disease which makes their skin intensely sensitive to sunlight. During the daytime, neither of them can ever go outdoors, or even come near a window. The disease makes their skin abnormally pale and icy cold to the touch. The very idea of touching Primeva fills me with horror. (Of course I didn't tell the count this.) Furthermore, all the wealth and fancy titles in the world would not be enough to make up for the anguish I would feel if my son—Barry Talmud, Jr.—had to enter the world with such a frightful handicap. But the second, and even more compelling, reason why I had to refuse Count Alucard, was that by this time I was head over heels in love with another woman.

Maria. Even now, thinking of her makes me tremble all over . . . I remember the magical moonlit night we met. The local gyspies were bitterly opposed to the tunnel, for reasons having to do with their ancient religion. One night they staged a torch-light procession up the mountain to the tunnel mouth. Hoping to reason with them I stepped forward to meet their leader, Madame Maria Openskya. I expected a wizened old crone, but to my amazement I found myself facing the most beautiful, the most fascinating, the most bewitching, the most—*everything*—woman I had ever met. And she was equally struck by me, or so I thought at the time.

She spoke English too! She'd lived for a time in New York, after her first husband, Anatol Openskya, died while spelunking in one of the Black Mountain caves—yet another mystical coincidence, for spelunking is my favorite pastime too. That night I addressed the gypsies and Maria interpreted for me.

With her help I pacified them. Soon they left and
Maria and I were alone, in the moonlight . . .

We were married just one month later. I left the
castle (the count was very nice and polite about it,
but I could tell he disapproved of my marrying a
gypsy), and Maria and I rented a little flat in the
nearby hamlet of New Pfalz. We were deliriously
happy together. During the day I had my work, in
the tunnel, and Maria had her fortunetelling, and
her gypsy friends, but the nights were full of love
and moonlight and magic . . .

My happiness ended suddenly and bitterly two
months ago when my contract came to an end and I
told Maria it was time for us to pack, to go back to
the States. Imagine my dismay when she informed
me she had no intention of ever leaving Transylvania
again.

"You're my wife," I told her, "whither I goest you
follow. And I'm going home." "No way," she replied,
"*This* is my home." "Be reasonable, Maria," I said.
"The tunnel is almost finished and there is no more
work for me in Transylvania. A man must work."
And she said, "We can live on my fortune-telling
income. Gypsy men don't work." We argued and
argued but she wouldn't give an inch, so finally I
said, with breaking heart, "In that case, Maria, I
must leave without you." She stood up to her full
height which is not very tall, and, her eyes blazing,
said (I'll never forget it): "You ain't goin' nowhere."

I stormed out of our former love nest and went
down to the station to wait for the train. But in the
morning when the train came in a crowd of armed
and menacing gypsies appeared out of the woods and
prevented me from boarding. The same thing

happened when I tried to hire a carriage, and when I attempted to flee on foot through the tunnel. Finally, under cover of darkness, I managed to escape their vigilance and made my way to Castle Alucard. You can imagine how embarrassed I felt at having to admit to Count Alucard that my marriage had failed and that I needed to hide from my wife! But he and Primeva took me in and promised to keep my whereabouts secret.

I've been hiding in a little room in a remote part of the castle. From Primeva—who usually brings me my tray—I've learned that Maria has begun divorce proceedings and obtained a court order preventing me from leaving the country, and that she's looking for me so she can serve the papers. How did it all turn so bad so fast?

As if I didn't have enough problems something awful has been happening to my skin. I think I must have picked up a fungus while spelunking. Thick coarse brown hair has begun growing all over my body, everywhere except the palms of my hands and the soles of my feet. There's so much hair on my face I look like a dog or a wolf! It doesn't help to shave because it grows right back, thicker. Lately Primeva's been hinting that she still likes me, hair and all, so I guess I could stay here and marry her, after the divorce, but I'd rather die. Sometimes, when the moon is full like it was the night I met Maria, I look out the window and howl . . .

There are other people living in the castle, but I don't feel I can trust any of them not to betray me to Maria, so I mostly hide in my room. The other day the housekeeper, Jane Morbidd, brought my evening tray. She was acting very strange, and I don't know if she can be trusted.

Last night I stepped out of my room for a minute, when a strange man suddenly opened the door of a room I had thought unoccupied. He introduced himself as Joseph Gawker, newly arrived to catalog the count's extensive library. He seemed a pleasant chap. I told him my name, and was shocked to learn from him that Maria was here, in the castle, looking for me, carrying papers. I was very distressed. Gawker was staring rather pointedly at the abundant hair on my face, so I muttered something about going away to shave and left him.

I spent the rest of the night in my room as usual, brooding about my doomed love for Maria, and worrying about the future. In the morning Mrs. Morbidd awoke me to tell me the newcomer, Joseph Gawker, had been found dead in suspicious circumstances. I wonder . . .

Madame Openskya

Madame Openskya is my name—it is true, I am married to Barry Talmud but we gypsies don't change our names just because of some man. Openskya I was born, and Openskya I will die.

I was born here, on Black Mountain. There have always been gypsies in Transylvania and the Openskyas have deep roots here, to the extent that a nomadic people can have roots anywhere. I married Anatol Openskya (no relation—all the Black Mountain gypsies are Openskyas), my childhood sweetheart, when I was fourteen, and we lived happily for many years. I learned the family trade, fortune telling, and prospered, and Anatol passed his time spelunking—exploring caves. Woman must work, man must have a hobby; it's the Openskya way.

Four years ago my Anatol was killed in a cave-in. A few months afterward I accepted an invitation from my aunt Sophie to come to New York City, in America, where she had an opening for an experienced fortune teller in the tea room she operated on Fifth Avenue. I accepted the invitation and the job and I lived in New York for two years. It helped me to forget my grief for Anatol but I was never happy there, and eventually I came back to Transylvania.

When I returned I found that the gypsies were in a turmoil because a great new railway tunnel was being built through Black Mountain, desecrating the gypsy homeland. The object is to connect Germany and Russia—did you ever hear such a stupid idea? A torchlight procession protesting the tunnel was planned, and naturally I volunteered to join.

It was the night of the full moon, I remember it well. As the procession reached the excavation site a tall man stepped forward and addressed us in English. As the only English-speaking gypsy, I became the spokeswoman. I sensed immediately that this man, Barry Talmud, far from being an enemy of the Openskyas was a potential ally. Also, I could see that he had fallen for me.

I told my people to go back to their tents, and for the rest of the night Barry and I talked. I explained the gypsy position and found him to be most sympathetic. He persuaded me that the tunnel would actually benefit us—he talked about employment, tax base, education, opportunities; all these things I do not understand. But then he showed me how the increased traffic would mean more business, as wealthy travellers passing through would wish their fortunes foretold. This I understand—after all, one Openskya telling the fortune of another Openskya, what future is there in this? Finally he suggested we gypsies open a tea room right next to the work camp, so the workmen could have their tea leaves read, and so forth, and we made a deal.

One month later we were married. We rented a little flat in New Pfalz as he was unwilling to live with me in my tent. It was the first indication that he and I, although soul mates, were not entirely compatible, and I should have heeded it. But I was in love.

Yes, of course I was in love. Do you think that I, an Openskya, would sell my body for a tea room? And we were happy together, Barry and me, deliriously happy. Like Anatol, Barry enjoyed spelunking, and I looked forward to the day when the tunnel was finished and Barry could spend his days digging about in Black Mountain's many caverns. I even hoped he would take my name, Openskya.

Boy, was I ever one stupid gypsy. Two months ago Barry informed me that he was taking me back to America. "No way," I told him, "This is my home." We argued back and forth, a thing I was not used to—gypsy men never talk back. They might hit you, but never argue. Barry didn't hit me but he never shut up either.

The upshot of it was, Barry walked out on me. On me! I wasn't going to let him get away, and when I told the rest of my people what had happened they agreed the Openskya honor was at stake. Gypsy gangs watched the train station, the tunnel, and the mountain passes, to prevent Barry Talmud's departure. Meanwhile the judge in New Pfalz, who is a client of mine, wrote up some legal papers that say that I am suing Barry for divorce and he can't leave Translyvania. Once I hand him this piece of paper—I have it here, in my apron—he'll have to stay.

Of course I don't want a divorce—the idea is unthinkable. I love Barry. I just want him to listen to reason, to realize that his destiny is here, with me.

Somehow Barry slipped through the net. For several weeks I didn't know where he was and I feared that he had escaped. Then a few days ago Jane Morbidd came and told me Barry was hiding in Castle Alucard. I knew this Morbidd woman when

I lived in New York—she was a client. I read the leaves for her and foretold trouble ahead—which was safe to say, since the woman was as jumpy as a cat. Trouble turned up so she's convinced I'm the real thing (which I am) and she's eager to keep on my good side. So she came and told me about Barry, and where he was hiding in the castle. She also told me he had hair growing all over his face and body, like a werewolf. I told her I'd placed a spell on Barry, and that so long as the hair wasn't growing out of the palms of his hands it was safe to be around him. And I gave the woman some wolfbane. Even though she's an American she's more superstitious than some of our dumb peasants! Between you and me I'd guess Barry picked up a fungus in one of the caves. Anatol used to have similar problems.

Yesterday Jane Morbidd snuck me into the castle through the servant's entrance. She gave me directions to the room where Barry was staying but I don't know how, I must have taken a wrong turn. When I got to the room I hid inside the armoire, papers in hand, figuring to pop out and surprise him. Well, the surprise was on me—when the door opened a total stranger was standing before me. I told him who I was and that I was looking for Barry—I was too startled to come up with a lie. Anyway, if the stranger gets word to Barry, it just might make him panic and try to flee the castle, right into the arms of the Openskyas!

After that I poked about the castle, trying to keep out of the way. At one point I glimpsed a young fellow wearing a nightshirt who looked so much like one of my clients back in New York. He was a writer, named Brick Newborn, and he interviewed me for a book he was writing. Could it possibly be the same man?

MADAME OPENSKYA

I slept for awhile in the kitchen, behind the stove. I was surprised to see Count Alucard come in on a midnight raid to get some food out of the larder. With all his money, you'd think he could hire someone to carry his trays! I took care he didn't see me. The Alucards and the Openskyas are enemies from way back—ever since one of my ancestors placed a curse on the family that makes them allergic to the sun. Or so the Alucards believe.

In the morning Jane told me that Joseph Gawker had been killed. I wasn't really surprised—this castle is an unhealthy place, and Gawker isn't the first traveler to meet his doom here. I'm looking forward to finding my sweetie, Barry, and taking him home to the safety of my tent.

Dr. Frankenfield with a needle

Dr. Rollo Frankenfield

Dr. Rollo Frankenfield, at your service. I started out as Ralph Frankenfield, but Rollo has more of a continental flavor, don't you agree? And strictly speaking, the Doctor bit is more of a courtesy title, if you know what I mean. Not that I didn't go to medical school, back in Boston; I just didn't finish. I flunked out, if the truth be told.

That was twenty years ago. Shortly after I left school I met a wealthy lady of a certain age who was more than convinced by my bedside manner. I accompanied her to Europe, as her personal physician, and haven't been back to the U.S. since. After she and I parted company, other ladies, all of them wealthy, most of them older, took her place. Dr. Frankenfield has done pretty well. My specialty is the skin— always a concern of the fairer sex.

Several years ago some of my ladies set me up in my own sanitarium in the south of France near Nice. It's a swell racket. The sanitarium is as comfortable as the finest hotel, and my ladies get every attention money can buy (including my own *personal* touch, if you know what I mean), and it does their skin a world of good.

Two years ago I met a young American woman who called herself Clara Whiteworthy—blond, pretty, no better than she should be. I'd been needing someone to distract the husbands of my ladies, and Clara was perfect for the job. I introduce her as my fiancée, a rich girl from a good family in Maryland, and we travel together as a team. I wouldn't say we had a romantic relationship—more one of convenience. We've slept together, but not very often in recent months.

Clara and I came to Transylvania five months ago. The count had heard about my sanitarium and he hoped I could help him. Count Alucard and all his family suffer from a rare hereditary disease in which the skin is highly sensitive to sunlight. The faintest rays cause him to break out into a hideous and painful rash, and he becomes violently ill. Because of this condition he and his daughter sleep all day in windowless rooms and only rise at night. They are excessively pale and their skin is cold and clammy to the touch. It would have been impossible for them to have traveled to France to visit my sanitarium.

The count and I corresponded and he became convinced that I could help him. He offered me a fully equipped lab at Castle Alucard, an assistant and all the money I could use. The timing was right for me— some rather sticky situations involving lawsuits had arisen in France—so Clara and I came here, to this life of weird luxury. It's an easy, pleasant life, in many ways. The lab is beautifully equipped and the count (who's an excellent chap, by the by) gets me everything I need. Eeyore, the assistant, is a former chemist who got messed up in a laboratory accident some years ago. Still, he's quite helpful and hard working, once you get used to his disfigurement.

The funny thing is, I think I may actually be on the verge of discovering something. There are animal oils that may just help human skin. Gee, I wish I'd paid more attention in school! In sheep, for instance, there's this lanolinic oil that's very promising. For the last few weeks I've had the Alucards on an exclusive diet of melted sheep fat. It's fairly disgusting stuff—the Alucards have taken to consuming it in private, away from the revolted eyes of other human beings—but I think I'm on to something. Wouldn't it be a kick if I really wasn't a fraud after all?

There are one or two problems with this setup. The worst is Lily Languish, the count's ward. This young girl arrived at the castle a year ago, apparently suffering the aftereffects of shock and smoke inhalation, following a fire which killed both her parents and destroyed her home. One of my duties is to treat her, but I can't figure out what the heck is wrong with her. She's too weak to walk, hardly eats, just sits there in her wheelchair, fainting away from time to time. And then there are those two mysterious wounds on her neck that won't heal. She has terrible nightmares, thrashes around so badly they have to tie her down. In some ways her symptoms suggest poisoning. I got some books on the subject from the count's library and I've been studying them, but I'm nowhere near the answer. My big fear is the girl will die on me, and then what? How will that make me look?

Another problem is Clara. She has no patience with me or my work. In public she's still civil enough but in private she won't give me the time of day. I can't remember the last time she paid a midnight visit to my bedchamber. (Which may be just as well—

lately another lady has been warming my bed . . .)
I've got a notion little Clara's got her eye on the
count. After all, the man's a widower, extremely
wealthy, generous. True, he's got a revolting skin
disease, but girls like Clara can't afford to be too
choosy. Why she must be pushing 28 by now!

I've no objection to Clara making goo goo eyes at
the count—who is blind to her charms, if you ask
me—but I don't like the way she's been running me
down lately. She's made no secret of the fact that
she doesn't think much of my scientific work. Last
night, for instance, when Eeyore came into the parlor
to tell me the results of the peach skin project, she
made a big show of trying to stop me from accompanying him. "Don't go," says she, "There are things here
on earth man was not meant to know." This was
aimed at the count, who is well known for his distaste
for the so called "black arts." I have enough problems,
I don't need that little chippie, Clara, talking against
me.

When I first came here I had the idea of getting
something going with Primeva, but I soon gave up.
The girl's a real witch—selfish, hot tempered, stuck
up. On more than one occasion she's just about come
out and accused me of being a quack! Luckily no one
likes her or pays her any attention. The count doesn't
say so but I think he fears she's a bit cracked.

The one person in this whole setup who is O.K. is
the housekeeper, Jane Morbidd. Believe it or not,
underneath that stern exterior dwells a woman of
warmth and passion. On certain cold nights, while
the Transylvanian winds whistled and howled about
the castle walls, little Jane has crept quietly into my
lonely bed . . . In company she's as dour and grim

with me as with everyone else, and we've scarcely exchanged more than a few words, in public *or* private.

Yesterday, when Joseph Gawker arrived, I got a bit of a shock. His brother Stephen, whom he strongly resembles, went to medical school with me. In fact, we were good friends and I visited the Gawker home in Binghamton one summer. Joseph was then but a lad. He might remember me—if he does he'd recall that I flunked out of medical school. *That* could queer my pitch. During dinner I caught him looking at me once or twice, but he didn't put it together.

There was a young American couple with us at dinner, the Newborns. As usual, Count Alucard and Primeva and Lily had retired early. The Newborns and Gawker did most of the talking during dinner, chatting about their travels. Clara was quiet—I guess she figured that neither Gawker nor Newborn was worth cultivating.

After dinner we all went our separate ways. I slept alone. In the morning Jane Morbidd woke me early, in great distress, to tell me that Joseph Gawker had died. I followed her to his room.

He was lying on his back beside the bed, dressed in his pajamas. From the way the bed covers were disarranged, I imagine he had been pulled out of the bed, whether before or after death I cannot say. His eyes and tongue were distended as though he'd been strangled or suffocated. There was a smell of garlic around his mouth. He was cold, as might be expected, for the window was wide open. Most strikingly, there were two wounds in his neck. These marks were the same size and similarly placed as Lily Languish's, but close examination revealed differences: Hers are a pair of individual punctures, with inflamed skin around them. On Gawker's neck there were two sets of crisscrossing shallow scratches.

I should mention that all the while I was making my examination, Jane Morbidd was standing in the doorway (she refused to enter the room), jumping up and down and shrieking some nonsense about vampires. It was finally necessary for me to smack her hard across the face, whereupon she came back to her senses and went about her duties, informing the Count and the other members of the household of Joseph Gawker's death.

I have no idea how long Joseph Gawker had been dead. As I've told you, I'm no doctor.

Clara Whiteworthy

Hello, pleased to make your acquaintance. Y'all make yourselves nice and comfy, hear? My name is Clara Whiteworthy and I'm from the eastern shore of Maryland, where my daddy breeds race horses. Do I *have* to tell y'all how old I am? Well, if you promise to keep it a deep dark secret, I'm twenty-four . . .

I've gotta tell the *real* truth here? Well in that case . . .

Cora Geckle's the name, born in Canarsie which is in Brooklyn, thirty-one years ago. When I was sixteen I met Boots Mulligan—you've probably heard of him. Boots taught me how to dress and fix my hair, and how to talk refined, and he taught me a lot of other things too. Boots had a real classy operation on the Bowery and I worked there for a number of years. After a while the life began to kinda pall so I took myself to Europe where I did pretty well, European gents being suckers for fresh-faced American girls, particularly blondes. I did all right, it was a living, but it still wasn't a future.

Two years ago I was in Paris, France, when I made the acquaintance of a gent named Dr. Rollo Frankenfield. Rollo had a swell scam going, passing himself off as a fancy doctor with a sanitarium in the south of France where rich old ladies went to have skin treatments. They—or their hubbies—paid through the nose for Rollo's services. Some of the hubbies weren't too pleased with the setup, so Rollo thought it'd be handy to have a blond-haired fiancée to distract from the fact that Rollo was romancing their wives. I fit the bill, so off we went to Nice.

The life there was O.K., it kept me in nice clothes and jewels, but I was beginning to feel like it wasn't leading anyplace when Rollo got invited to come here, to Transylvania. Somehow Count Alucard had heard about Rollo's skin treatments—I don't know how because I never heard of Rollo curing anybody of anything. The count and his daughter have a skin disease that makes it impossible for them to go outdoors, so since they couldn't go to France they wanted Rollo to come here. Well, Rollo was eager to leave because some kinda sticky situations were developing around then. And I decided to come along for the ride—I'd never lived in a castle and I thought it might improve my luck.

We've been here now for five months. It's a restful place, not much night life, just the same people every day. The count is a really fine gent. He has wonderful manners and he's real cultured—classy. Primeva is so different you'd never guess she was his daughter. Mean as a snake and rude too. She hasn't had a civil word for either me or Rollo since we came here, and just about accused us of being con artists! Then there's Lily—she's the count's ward, a helpless little invalid. I might feel sorry for her except she's just as stuck up as Primeva.

There are also two servants. Eeyore is the handyman, besides which he helps Rollo in the lab. Rollo doesn't mind him but he gives me the willies. He's horribly deformed and he's always muttering and giving me dirty looks. I avoid him.

Jane Morbidd is the housekeeper. I don't recall making her acquaintance previously but she does, which is unfortunate. Soon after we came here Jane Morbidd came to my room to tell me she remembered me from my Cora Geckle days, when I was working in Boots's Bowery establishment. I tried to tough it out but I could see she had the goods on me. And she had a proposition, which I was not surprised to hear about. If I would pay her off she'd keep mum, otherwise she'd tell Rollo and the count and anybody else who cared to hear it, that I was Cora Geckle and so forth. I went along with it. I could have got on the train and gone back to Paris, France, or someplace else, but I was tired from the trip, and everything. And the money she was asking for wasn't that much.

But the main reason I decided to stay was that the minute I laid eyes on Castle Alucard I knew I'd found the pot of gold at the end of the rainbow. It is my desire to become the second Countess Vladimir Alucard! It's true Vlad (I don't call him that yet, of course, but it's how I think of him) has a dreadful hereditary skin disease, but who among us is perfect? Vlad is very very wealthy, besides being kind and wise and tall and well-educated, and I know I could make him a fine wife.. And mother to his children. (As for *that* part of marriage, after the Bowery, Vlad's skin disease doesn't look that bad, believe me.)

Raising the money to pay off Jane Morbidd was a problem until I discovered a swell resource right here in the castle—namely the old books in the library. There's a dealer in Budapest who buys them from me—I gave him a list of what's available and he tells me what he wants and when he wants it. Kinda like the New York Public Library, only private. I go to Budapest every month or so on the excuse that I'm buying clothes, but instead I'm selling books. A girl's gotta do what a girl's gotta do.

As for my relations with Rollo, they're what you think they are, except we don't do it much any more. We've kinda grown apart. Rollo's begun to believe his own lies, which is the kiss of death in this game. He spends all his time in the lab, with that freak Eeyore, cooking up weird messes. He thinks he can cure Vlad and Primeva with sheepfat, of all things. It smells bad and when I become Countess Alucard I'll put a stop to it. Sooner, I hope. Lately I've been trying to put a wedge between Vlad and Rollo. I know Vlad is too much of a gent to make a pass at another man's fiancée, so in a subtle kinda way I'm trying to get him to start asking questions about Rollo, *without* asking questions about me. Tricky. See, if I broke up with Rollo I'd have to be the one to leave, which I don't want. One thing I'm doing is to plant the idea that Rollo and Eeyore are up to no good, down in that lab. Vlad hates and despises witchcraft and superstition and black magic and is determined to stamp it out, which is an uphill task seeing as Transylvania is full of folk who feel otherwise.

Yesterday in the parlor when I met Joseph Gawker, at first I thought he might be a scientist, here to study Rollo's work. When I learned he was a librarian I was kinda taken aback, as you may imagine. When I got a minute alone with Vlad I asked him to arrange a carriage so I could go to Budapest today—I thought I might get some of the books back, or borrow substitutes. Now of course I don't have to go.

There were two other newcomers last night, a young American couple named Brick and Giddy Newborn. They and Gawker joined Rollo and me for dinner, which made for a livelier evening than usual. Lily and the Alucards had left our company before dinner, like always.

After dinner I went up to my room alone. There were some books that I'd taken from the library and I decided to try to sneak them back onto the shelves, because Joseph Gawker had been telling everyone that he was going to work first thing in the morning. But when I peeked into the library Gawker was in there already. He didn't see me so I tiptoed back to my room. I put my hair up and creamed my face and went to bed.

In the morning Jane Morbidd came banging on my door to tell me Joseph Gawker had been found dead, under mysterious circumstances that suggested vampires! I was shocked and also kinda relieved, because now maybe I don't have to worry about the missing books.

Eeyore

Eeyore

Call me Eeyore. I used to have more names before the explosion but I lost them. I was born near here, in Transylvania. I went to university in Germany and Scotland and I became a chemist, a brilliant chemist—not as brilliant as I am now, of course.

The explosion that changed my life happened seven years ago. I was working in a laboratory somewhere—it doesn't matter where—and everything blew up. The explosion created terrible fumes that got into my brain and rearranged the cells and made me a genius! My body is different too. I don't walk as well as I used to, and I twitch sometimes. What no one else knows is that I can climb like a monkey. I have phenomenal strength in my hands and arms and a complete lack of fear. I can climb the castle walls as easily as a spider. I could probably fly if I put my mind to it.

Another change, since the accident, is that I look different. Some people are afraid of me and laugh at me. I don't care. When I'm emperor of the world all the people who laughed at me will have to go to the South Pole and work in the ice cream factories.

But not Count Alucard—when I take over I'll let him stay. After the explosion, when everyone wanted to lock me up in an institution for the mentally handicapped (Me!), he asked me to come to Castle Alucard to work as a handyman. When I'm emperor I'll let him be the handyman, here in my castle.

Another person I like is Miss Lily. Everyone thinks she's a sicky too, but I know how smart she is. In nice weather I push her wheelchair around the gardens and I talk to her. She's the only one who knows my plan.

Here's how I'm going to take over the world: I'm going to *repeat* the experiment that went wrong seven years ago, but this time I'm going to catch the fumes in canisters and seal them up! Soon the railway tunnel through Black Mountain will be completed and the first passenger train will go through. I'll open the canisters and release the fumes inside the tunnel, and when the train comes out the other side everyone on it will be my slave. Then they will go out into the world with more canisters of fumes and enslave other people. Just the way vampires make more vampires, in the old legends.

I've been working on this plan for two years, ever since Barry Talmud arrived. I listened to him talking with the count and I learned he was an American railway engineer, brought here by the Transylvania Transit Authority to construct the tunnel. That's when I got the idea.

Then, five months ago, the rest of the plan fell into place. Dr. Rollo Frankenfield came to stay, doing some sort of experiments on skin. The count set up a laboratory for him and suggested that I could be his assistant. Little did he know that a lab was the one thing I lacked! (The doctor's experiments have no bearing on my work—he's constantly melting

sheep fat and making other disgusting messes, and
if you ask me he's no true scientist.) Now that I have
access to a lab, it's just a matter of assembling the
right chemicals and duplicating the experiment. My
only problem is that it was so long ago I can't
remember. There was sulphur, chloroform—I've
begun assembling ingredients as I recall them, but
I have trouble remembering and every time I try to
make a list I get a headache . . .

I'll tell you everything that happened last night,
but then I have to get back to my work. I had heard
from Dr. Frankenfield that a newcomer had arrived
at the castle, a librarian named Joseph Gawker.
Naturally I was curious so, just before sunset, I
climbed out my window and ascended the castle wall
to Gawker's window. Unseen I watched the man ad-
just his cravat in the mirror, confirming my fears.
This was no librarian—it was Dr. Stephen Gawker
who used to work at the asylum near here. Had he
learned of my plans for conquering the world, and
come to take me away?

I worried about Gawker as I climbed down the
castle wall to the laboratory, but then I forgot about
him in my absorption in the task at hand. Dr.
Frankenfield had been experimenting on peach skin.
Now as I looked through the microscope I saw that
a furry gray fungus was growing on the specimen. I
went up to the parlor to inform the doctor of this
development.

They were all there, gathered around the fireplace: The count; Miss Lily; the count's daughter,
Primeva (she's really mean to me—when I become
emperor I'm going to feed her to the slugs); the doctor;
his fiancée, Clara Whiteworthy, who is also my

enemy; and Gawker. I made a face at him so he wouldn't recognize me and I spoke to Dr. Frankenfield.

"Come to the lab with me, master," said I. "It lives." (The doctor insists that I call him "master"—won't he be surprised when the shoe is on the other foot!) Miss Whiteworthy tried to detain him but he joined me at the door. Just as we were leaving, the housekeeper, Jane Morbidd (soon to become slug food), arrived with some people who'd gotten lost in the woods. I never did meet them.

The doctor and I worked in the lab for a while, and then Mrs. Morbidd came to take him to dinner. I kept on working until very late. I kept trying to remember—was it TNT? DDT? When I finally stopped work I went up to the library to get a book. I like to look at the pictures in science books when I have trouble sleeping. But *he* was there, Gawker, so I crept away (he didn't see me), and went down to my little room in the cellar. On the way, I saw Clara Whiteworthy slinking along with an armful of books, but she didn't see me.

This morning I was in the lab when Mrs. Morbidd told me Gawker was dead. I laughed and laughed and laughed.

Lily Languish

My name is Lily Languish. I'll do my best to tell you everything I know. I don't know very much because I'm an invalid—I just sit here in my wheelchair and I hardly ever get out, and no one talks to me much. You'll have to excuse me if I drop off. I faint a lot these days . . .

I'm twenty-two years old. Until last year I lived with my darling Mummy and Daddy in a beautiful house in Happy Valley, which is in a nice part of Transylvania, not like this. Then there was that terrible night . . .

Lightning struck our house and there was a terrible fire and I almost died, and Mummy and Daddy did die. When I came out of the coma I was here, in Castle Alucard. In Daddy's will he said that if anything should happen to him his friend, Count Alucard, was to look after me until I become twenty-five, when I'll inherit the Languish estates.

I sometimes wonder if I'll ever live to be twenty-five. Ever since the fire I've been ill. I can hardly walk at all, I'm so weak, and I have no appetite. I've lost so much weight none of my dresses fits any more. Who would believe I used to be captain of the hockey team at school? I have terrible nightmares every night, about the fire and—other things. I toss and turn so much I have to be strapped in so I won't fall out of bed. The worst thing of all is these marks on my neck. I began noticing them a few months after I came here. They're little puncture wounds about an inch apart, and they *don't heal*. I was beginning to get well before the marks appeared, but since then I've been getting worse and worse.

One of the things I have bad dreams about is Eeyore. He's sort of a handyman around here. He used to be a chemist but he was in an awful explosion and now he's horribly disfigured, and he twitches and says strange things. I guess I should feel sorry for him because he's suffered like me, but he just gives me the *creeps*. Sometimes he pushes my wheelchair around the garden, and he jabbers on and on about his mad schemes—taking over the world with *chemistry*—but I don't listen. And a couple of times I swear I saw him looking in at me through the window. But that's not possible, is it, since my window is way up high over the moat?

The count, Uncle Vladimir, also gives me the creeps. He's very good and kind I know, but he's got this awful skin disease that makes him look really icky. When I first came here he sort of hinted that he was interested in me, marriage-wise. The very thought makes me ill! Then there's Primeva. She's really mean and spiteful to me, especially when we're alone. I'm afraid of her. And Mrs. Morbidd, the housekeeper—she's a cheeky one! She certainly doesn't do much of a job of looking after this castle—the place is a *disgrace*. Uncle Vladimir sure keeps some strange people around him. There was an American railway engineer here, named Barry Talmud, who seemed like a decent sort, but then he fell madly in love with one of the local gypsies.

When I heard that a doctor was coming to look after me I hoped he'd be able to cure me, but Dr. Frankenfield seems just as mystified by my condition as everyone else. I don't think much of him, or his fiancée, Clara Whiteworthy. She puts on airs and brags about her wealthy family but she doesn't fool me. Riffraff, all of them. Daddy *never* would have put up with it.

I was in the parlor last night, as usual, with Uncle Vladimir, Primeva, the doctor and Miss Whiteworthy, when the new librarian, Joseph Gawker, came in. I was so shocked! There was a doctor, Stephen Gawker, who worked in the asylum nearby for several years. When the fire broke out, a year ago, Dr. Gawker was the one who treated my parents. I don't remember, of course, because I was unconscious, but everyone said it was his fault that Mummy and Daddy died. Because of that, the doctor lost his job and had to leave Transylvania. And now here's Joseph Gawker who looks so much like him— they must be brothers! I was so shocked to see him . . .

I'm sorry, did I faint again? There's not much more to tell. A young couple from America, the Newborns, also arrived last night. Soon afterward Uncle Vladimir and Primeva and I retired, leaving the others to have their dinner. The Alucards don't like to eat with other people because Dr. Frankenfield has them on some icky diet and it's too disgusting to watch. I just wasn't hungry, I never am. Uncle Vladimir picked me up and carried me upstairs and tucked me in and buckled the straps around me like he always does. I had awful nightmares, as usual. Then in the morning Mrs. Morbidd woke me up to tell me Joseph Gawker had been killed. All I could think was, if he's anything like his brother it serves him right . . .

Primeva under interrogation

Primeva

No, you may *not* call me Primeva—Miss Alucard, if you please. When my father, Count Alucard, dies, I will inherit the title and the castle and the lands and the serfs, and then I will be Countess Alucard. That is, unless he makes the unthinkable error of remarrying and spawning a male Alucard.

My mother, Countess Vera, died when I was born, twenty-nine year ago. Shortly before that, father's older brother, Count Perffy, died in a fire, along with his family. So I am the last of the line. When I marry—if I marry—my children will take the Alucard name. This is how we do things here in Transylvania. Much as I respect father, it is unquestionable that I will run things far better than he. He is weak-minded, full of sentimental notions about improving the peasant's lot. Education, railroads, social welfare—rot, all of it! I look forward to a return to the traditional ways, to re-establishing the happy mutual respect between master and slave that such practices as flogging, for example, engender.

I, like my father and most of our ancestors, suffer from a rare, if not unique affliction. Our skin is so exquisitely sensitive to sunlight that we dare not venture out of doors during the day. As you may have observed, my skin is extraordinarily pale, and should you touch me (which I would not permit) you would find that my flesh is very cold indeed. This remarkable condition has given rise to the rumor that we Alucards are vampires! I see no reason to discourage this notion, as it can only strengthen the hold that the Alucard name has over the ignorant peasantry.

Because of the Alucard affliction we rarely leave the castle. Father educated me at home; he has an extensive library and is very learned. We always speak English, which father thinks of as the language of reason and progress. (Personally I would chose Hungarian, or Russian.) He is particularly fond of Americans, always inviting them to visit. Our housekeeper, Mrs. Jane Morbidd, is a case in point; the woman is incompetent, uncouth, lazy, and a bad cook. She arrived here three years ago looking for work, her only qualification being that she was American. Father hired her on the spot and won't hear a word against her. Have you ever seen a dustier castle?

Barry Talmud was another of father's Americans, although in his case father's trust was justified. Mr. Talmud is a railway engineer. He stayed with us for several months when he first came to Transylvania, two years ago, and both father and I thought he might make a fitting consort for me. True, he does not have aristocratic blood, but he is healthy, intelligent and well-mannered. There is much to be said for grafting sturdy young stock on to an old bloodline. Father and I were appalled when Mr. Talmud became infatuated with a local gypsy, Maria Openskya, and married her. But the marriage ended (not surprisingly) and two months ago Mr. Talmud returned, in great distress, asking to hide in the castle. Father and I took him in and gave him a room in an empty wing of the castle. I've been taking food to him. He picked up a fungus somewhere that's caused hair to grow all over his face and body, and he seems to be very upset by it. It doesn't bother me in the least, and I have hopes that soon Mr. Talmud will forget about his gypsy and will realize how advantageous it would be for him to marry me.

The so-called Dr. Frankenfield and his alleged fiancée, Clara Whiteworthy, are a good example of my father's habit of collecting American riffraff. Frankenfield was running a sanitorium in the south of France for the treatment of skin diseases. Father corresponded with him and became convinced the man could cure us and invited him here. He arrived with Miss Whiteworthy five months ago. Both of them are clearly frauds, which I've told my father, but he won't listen. He gave Frankenfield the run of the castle, a handsome salary, and an expensively equipped laboratory, with our handyman, Eeyore, as lab assistant. (Eeyore is another waif—this time not American but local. He studied to be a chemist but he was in an accident that left him crippled and totally deranged. Of *course* father took the man in.)

Lately Frankenfield has had father and me on a diet of sheep fat, and nothing else. Father is very enthusiastic about this cure. I'm skeptical. To tell the truth, I'm not that eager to be cured. I have no desire to ever leave the castle or go out in daylight. And I'd hate to have pink cheeks and freckles like Clara Whiteworthy. It may sound vain to say it but I'm beautiful as I am!

The other member of the household is Lily Languish. She's my father's ward and she's been here for a year, ever since her parents died. She was very sick when she first arrived, but gradually began to recover. It was then that I realized father was nursing a romantic interest in her! I was horrified, as you may well imagine. Lily is a good thirty years younger than father. It's true she comes from a good family but you could hardly call the Languishes nobility. She's just a simpering little school girl—the idea of her becoming Countess Alucard, and being my step-mother, and making a male baby that would grow up to be Count Alucard—why it's utterly *absurd*. Out of the question!

I had to nip this in the bud. I did not grow up in Transylvania for nothing. From my nanny who was a local peasant with a well-earned reputation as a witch, I learned many useful arts. I have a garden on one of the battlements, which I tend by moonlight. There I grow various things—herbs, mushrooms and the like. By adding a tiny pinch of a deadly mushroom to Lily's porridge, I can cause her to have such dreadful nightmares that she must be strapped in at night, else she will injure herself. I hoped the nightmares would be enough to convince father that Lily was not countess material, but no. He took to strapping her to her bed at night so she wouldn't harm herself, and from the tender way he tightened the buckles I realized he was still smitten. This was six months ago.

Next I concocted a potent herbal brew from a traditional recipe. Its effect is to cause weakness, fainting, loss of appetite. I filled a hypodermic syringe with it and entered Lily's room. She was strapped to the bed, sleeping. As I stood over her, syringe in hand wondering where to place the needle, inspiration struck. With the needle I made two little holes in her neck, just like in the old vampire legends, and injected the drug into them. My scheme worked brilliantly. I give Lily the mushrooms about once a week, the injections every other night. The effect has been to turn Lily into a chronic invalid, an object of pity to my father, rather than love.

But even more effective than the drugs are the little vampire marks. Half of Transylvania now believes Lily to be a vampire. Father himself believes it! This is my father's deepest secret—much as he pretends to scorn superstition and admire progress, he's really as frightened of ghosts and werewolves as the most ignorant serf in Transylvania.

I spent yesterday as usual sleeping in my windowless bed chamber. After sunset I met with my father, Lily, Frankenfield, and Miss Whiteworthy in the parlor. We were joined there first by Joseph Gawker, a librarian (from America, wouldn't you know?) who father had hired to catalog the books, and then by a young couple named Newborn who'd become lost in the woods. I only exchanged a few words with Gawker. As I recall, he took my hand and, finding it cold, suggested I drink wine. I told him that I didn't drink—it's one of the aspects of the Alucard affliction; we can't tolerate alcohol. Soon afterward Mrs. Morbidd signalled that dinner was about to be served. Ever since father and I have been on this sheep fat regimen we don't eat dinner with the others—people find it too disgusting to watch. And Lily is seldom strong enough to sit through dinner. So father picked Lily up out of her wheelchair and, with me following, went upstairs. I watched as he strapped Lily in and then we said goodnight and parted.

I spent the long night in my usual fashion—played some solitare, read a bit, tended my garden. About two hours after Lily had gone to bed I crept into her room to give her an injection. On the way back I was startled to glimpse Mr. Gawker, apparently on the way up to his room. I hope he didn't see me—and if he did, that he didn't notice the hypodemic in my hand.

I was just preparing for bed this morning when Mrs. Morbidd came in to tell me about Gawker's death. So I guess it doesn't matter whether he saw me or not, does it?

Count Alucard

Welcome, welcome to Castle Alucard. I hope you are comfortable. Forgive me, but I must keep the blinds tightly closed as I am violently allergic to the rays of the sun. It is the curse of the Alucard family, this hereditary affliction. My father had it, Primeva has it, my brother Perffy . . .

Ah, Perffy. You have probably been told that Perffy died in a fire, with his wife and child. This I must now confess is not true. Perffy lives—hopelessly insane, little more than a groveling, drooling madman, but yet: He lives! Heir to this fiefdom, rightful Count Alucard, father of Primeva—may God forgive me, Perffy lives. And I am his usurper.

I shall begin at the beginning.

My older brother Perffy was always a difficult boy. He was fond of schoolboy pranks—putting spiders in the housemaid's knickers; teasing cats by pulling out their whiskers; dropping stones over the battlements on the peasants; that sort of thing. I remember once he found a nest of baby vipers and released them in mother's knitting basket. As he grew older the pranks became less amusing and there were problems with the law. Finally it became necessary to incarcerate him in the asylum at Happy Valley. He soon recovered, or so it seemed, helped by a young

Count Alucard in a dungeon

American nurse, Alexis Strick, with whom he fell in love. Mother and father were opposed to this union, on dynastic grounds, but their objections were overruled by events when a balcony on which they were standing collapsed and they were both killed. (Perffy was close by at the time, and although I was not then suspicious, I am now convinced he killed them.)

Perffy, now Count Alucard, married Alexis and they soon produced a daughter. I was at the time happily married to my second cousin, Lady Vera, who was expecting a child. Tragedy struck one dark stormy night when, alerted by Alexis's blood curdling screams I rushed to my window where I witnessed my brother hacking her to death with that same battle-axe with which my ancestor, Vlad the Magnificent, subdued the Visigoths. It was too late to save Alexis. With the help of a trusted servant, Dargon, I restrained Perffy and we carried him to the east wing of the castle, where my grandfather had providentially built a dungeon. Leaving Dargon to keep guard I returned to my chamber only to find my beloved Vera breathing her last. The night's terrors had induced premature labor, and both she and the unborn child perished.

It was not until many hours later that I thought of baby Primeva. Expecting the worst I entered the nursery, where I found her babbling happily in her crib, playing with her pet rat. I decided then and there what I must do.

Dargon and I set a bonfire in the courtyard, which consumed Alexis's remains. The villagers saw the flames and smoke, and the next day learned that Perffy with his wife and daughter, had perished in a fire. Perffy had never been well-loved, so the peasants were happy to accept me as his successor. Shortly afterward it was announced that Vera had died leaving me with a daughter. Since all of Transylvania knows of the affliction that curses our family, no one wondered that baby Primeva was not shown off to the populace.

Dargon and the other servants who knew the truth are all dead now. For the past five years I have been caring for Perffy myself. He is much deteriorated—he spends most of his time lying on the stone floor of his cell watching the spiders. He barely looks up when I bring his tray, which I do every night after the rest of the household has retired.

The terrible events of that night have left me an unhappy, even tormented man. I still hear Alexis's screams, Vera's sighs, Perffy's grunts. I ask myself— could it have turned out differently? The knowledge that I am living a lie, that I am not the true Count Alucard, haunts me.

I have tried to be a good father to Primeva. As the poor girl shares the terrible Alucard skin disease, her life has been limited to this castle. I've educated her myself, hoping to stir a love of science and progress and light, in place of those dark preoccupations which, alas, have such a potent hold over the Transylvanian soul. I cannot say that I've been successful. She's a difficult girl, strong-willed, tempestuous; almost, dare I say it, like her father.

My primary concern, as an Alucard, must be to continue the line. Primeva will inherit the title after my death, of course, but then what? A few years ago, when the young railway engineer, Barry Talmud, came to Transylvania, I entertained hopes that he might make a good husband for her. I know, the man is untitled, a nobody, but it might have been not so bad an idea to add a little fresh blood to the family tree. And he is educated, a scientist almost. Most important, he was available—very few eligible bachelors turn up at Transylvania Station. And Primeva liked him. Alas, all our hopes came to nothing for the man fell madly in love with one of the local gypsies and married her. Recently the marriage has foundered and the man is here at Castle Alucard, hiding from his gypsy wife. I am glad to provide a refuge for him.

As you may have noticed, this castle is home to several other unfortunates. Seven years ago Eeyore, the son of my faithful old servant Dargon, was injured in a laboratory explosion, ending a promising career as a chemist. Having sponsored Eeyore's education, I now offered him a home and a livelihood, as handyman here at Castle Alucard. He is a little odd, but quite harmless. Mrs. Jane Morbidd arrived at the door three years ago. An American, she was penniless and far from home. I saw immediately that although she had hit hard times she was an honest, industrious woman, and hired her on the spot to be housekeeper. I pride myself on being a good judge of character.

Dear little Lily Languish joined my household one year ago, after the tragic accident that claimed both her parents' lives. Louis Languish, her father, was a friend and fellow landowner, and in his will named me his executor and Lily's guardian. In the long months while Lily languished, fighting for her life, I became very fond of her. Even, I admit, to the point of hoping to marry her. I know, I am a great deal older than she. But she is a frail creature—perhaps more suited to the tender embraces of a mature man than the rough passions of one her own age . . . Also, I had by then begun to despair of Primeva's ever marrying and producing an heir to continue the line.

Sad to say, Lily's health has not flourished. Six months ago I first noticed on her white neck, two small red marks. At about this time her health took a downward turn—her nightmares, always bad, intensified (indeed, I must strap her to her bed at night to prevent her from injuring herself), and she grew so weak that she had to be confined to a wheelchair. And the scars have not healed. I shudder when I see them for I know that in these mountains legends of—I can't say the word, it begins with a "V"—are rife. Poor Lily Languish!

Dr. Frankenfield and Miss Clara Whiteworthy, his fiancée, have been with us for five months. Dr. Frankenfield is a distinguished medical man, a specialist in diseases of the skin. I brought him here in hopes that he would find a cure for the dreadful skin ailment that afflicts the Alucards. And I hoped that he would be of help to poor Lily. Alas, he has not been able to do much for her (although he has an idea now, unlikely though it seems, that she is being poisoned!), but he has made brilliant progress in the lab, assisted by Eeyore. I love to go down there and watch the retorts bubbling and stewing. Recently the doctor has put Primeva and me on an exclusive diet of sheep fat. It is disgusting to eat but I have hope that it will help us. Dr. Frankenfield, in addition to his professional skills, is an enjoyable companion, full of amusing stories. I do like Americans—their energy, their optimism. The girl, Miss Whiteworthy, is pleasant enough, although common.

Yesterday after I arose at dusk, Mrs. Morbidd told me that Joseph Gawker had arrived. I had been expecting him for some time. He is a librarian and I had engaged him to catalog my library. (I inherited a vast library, full of quaint and curious volumes of forgotten lore, and I have long dreamed of putting it in order according to the newfangled decimal system.) I met Mr. Gawker in the parlor, and chatted briefly with him, finding him to be a fine young man. I introduced him to the other members of the household. A few minutes later Mrs. Morbidd returned with a young couple, Brick and Giddy Newborn, who had become lost in the woods near the castle. Naturally I offered them a room.

Soon afterward I retired with Lily and Primeva, leaving our healthy American guests to enjoy their dinner away from the gloomy spectacle of illness. I carried Lily to her room and strapped her in, then said goodnight to her and Primeva. Later, when all was quiet I brought Perffy his tray, as usual.

I spent the rest of the night in lonely contemplation. Something was bothering me—something to do with the evening's arrivals, but I couldn't think what. I paced back and forth through the night, finally interrupted by the arrival of Jane Morbidd with the disquieting news that Joseph Gawker had been found dead, under highly mysterious circumstances. She was hysterical, so I discount her report that there were marks on his neck . . .

The Quiz

PART I:

Match the quotation with the character

1. "I pride myself on being a good judge of character"
2. "A girl's gotta do what a girl's gotta do"
3. "Gee, I wish I'd paid more attention in school"
4. "Looking back, I think he was a practised seducer"
5. "Housework is not what you'd call my *forte*"
6. "I look forward to a return of the traditional ways"
7. "sometimes . . . I look out my window and howl"
8. "Who would believe I used to be captain of the hockey team at school"
9. "I could probably fly if I put my mind to it"
10. "Woman must work, man must have a hobby"
11. "This whole business is far too much like a Morglu Clump story for my taste"

a. Mrs. Jane Morbidd
b. Brick Newborn
c. Giddy Newborn
d. Barry Talmud
e. Maria Openskya
f. Dr. Frankenfield
g. Clara Whiteworthy
h. Eeyore
i. Lily Languish
j. Primeva Alucard
k. Count Alucard

109

PART II: Multiple Choice

1. What did Joseph see in the window of his room?
   a. An old gypsy
   b. A bat
   c. A vampire
   d. Eeyore

2. Who knew in advance of Joseph Gawker's arrival?
   a. Count Alucard
   b. The count and the housekeeper, Mrs. Morbidd
   c. The count, Mrs. Morbidd, and Primeva
   d. Nobody

3. What is Giddy Newborn's guilty secret?
   a. She and Primeva are first cousins
   b. She's been stealing books from the library
   c. She had a premarital affair with Joseph Gawker's brother, Stephen
   d. She spied Count Alucard carrying a tray of food upstairs

4. What is Eeyore's plan?
   a. He wants to blow up the tunnel through Black Mountain
   b. He wants to recreate the explosion in which he was injured, then capture the fumes and use them to enslave people
   c. He wants to create a race of vampires
   d. He wants to marry Lily Languish

5. Why did the Newborns come to Transylvania on their honeymoon?
    a. Brick was researching a horror novel he was writing
    b. Giddy was curious about the romantic land where her aunt Alexis had lived
    c. Giddy was looking for Stephen Gawker
    d. Giddy hoped to prove that she was heiress to the Alucard lands

6. While Maria Openskya was in New York City, she met: (you may check more than one answer)
    a. Clara Whiteworthy, aka Cora Geckle
    b. Jane Morbidd
    c. Brick Newborn
    d. Joseph Gawker

7. Why does Jane Morbidd wear wolfbane?
    a. To protect herself from Eeyore
    b. To protect herself from becoming a vampire
    c. To protect herself from Barry Talmud
    d. To protect herself from Perffy

8. Why is Barry Talmud unable to leave Transylvania?
    a. Maria Openskya has cast a spell upon him
    b. He *believes* Maria Openskya has cast a spell on him
    c. He has contracted a fungal disease while exploring caves
    d. The Openskyas are watching all the roads and passes to prevent his departure

9. Which of these couples is conducting a secret illicit affair (you may check more than one answer)?
    a. Dr. Frankenfield and Jane Morbidd
    b. Count Alucard and Lily Languish
    c. Count Alucard and Clara Whiteworthy
    d. Barry Talmud and Primeva Alucard

10. What's wrong with Lily Languish?
    a. Eeyore is performing experiments on her
    b. Clara Whiteworthy is poisoning her because she fears the count wants to marry her
    c. Primeva is poisoning her because she fears the count wants to marry her
    d. Dr. Frankenfield is purposefully letting her die

11. What reason does Dr. Frankenfield have to fear Joseph Gawker?
    a. Gawker might notice the missing books and connect them with Frankenfield
    b. Gawker might recognize Frankenfield as a former medical student who flunked out of school
    c. Gawker might recognize Clara Whiteworthy as a former prostitute
    d. Gawker might accuse Frankenfield of malpractice, in connection with the deaths of Lily Languish's parents

12. What is Clara Whiteworthy's goal?
    a. To save enough money to get back to New York
    b. To get the goods on Jane Morbidd, and stop being blackmailed
    c. To marry Count Alucard
    d. To get Dr. Frankenfield to leave Transylvania and take her back to France

13. What is Count Alucard's guilty secret?
    a. He murdered his brother, Perffy
    b. He is Eeyore's father
    c. He has been sleeping with Lily Languish while she was drugged
    d. He is not really the count

PART III: True or False

1. Count Alucard recognized Giddy Newborn as his late sister-in-law, Alexis's, niece
2. Joseph Gawker's body was found in the library
3. Joseph Gawker saw Primeva carrying the syringe
4. The servant, Dargon, was Eeyore's father
5. Dr. Frankenfield hopes to cure Lily Languish with sheepfat
6. Neither Maria Openskya nor Barry Talmud wants a divorce
7. Joseph Gawker told Barry Talmud about seeing Maria Openskya
8. Brick Newborn recognized Castle Alucard from Stephen Gawker's descriptions
9. Jane Morbidd is blackmailing Primeva
10. Count Alucard thinks Clara Whiteworthy is "common"

PART IV. Whodunnit

1. Which of the suspects killed Joseph Gawker?

2. What was his/her motive?

The Truth

What a good man Count Vladimir Alucard is! Growing up with a rare disease that affects almost all members of his family and makes it impossible for any of them to ever be in direct sunlight, the count nevertheless became a decent, socially-responsible aristocrat. With, however, one guilty secret.

He isn't the real count. His mad older brother, Perffy Alucard, who was often kept in the local insane asylum in his youth because of violent episodes, was free and at home when a castle balcony collapsed, killing both their parents and making Perffy, then 26, the new count. Twenty-two year old Vladimir suspected Perffy had murdered their parents, but couldn't prove it.

A little later, Perffy married a nurse from the insane asylum, an American woman named Alexis Strick, and they had a daughter, Primeva. A few months after Primeva's birth, Perffy murdered his wife, horribly, with an axe. Vladimir's pregnant wife died from the shock. Vladimir, with the help of trusted servants, subdued Perffy and locked him away in an attic room, where he has been ever since. The last of the servants who knew about Perffy died years ago; now, the count is the only one in the house who knows he even exists. He brings Perffy all his food himself, up to his cell in the attic.

Primeva has no idea Vladimir isn't her real father. Her pride and short temper she's inherited from Perffy, along with the family illness. And it's probably Perffy's wild streak that has led to her treatment of Lily Languish, the count's ward.

Lily Languish moved to the castle a year ago, after lightning struck her home and caused the fire in which she suffered shock and smoke inhalation, and in which her parents died, apparently partly because of the bungling of one Dr. Stephen Gawker, an American physician working at that same local insane asylum, who had happened to be the first medical man on the scene. The scandal of Gawker's failure led to his dismissal from the asylum and later departure from the country.

Lily's parents, wealthy landowners in the area, had been friends of Vladimir's, and made Lily his ward. When Lily was well enough to leave the hospital, Vladimir brought her to Castle Alucard to recover. Primeva saw that her father's tender interest in Lily was becoming too tender, that he was actually considering a proposal of marriage. Primeva, fearing she would lose her inheritance, has been systematically poisoning Lily. Since some of the castle servants, and other locals, believe in vampires, and it would be impossible to make the poison injections without leaving any mark, Primeva has deliberately made two vampire-like wounds, to confuse and baffle diagnosis. Also, she knows the suggestion of vampirism would repel Count Alucard.

Among those who most thoroughly believe in vampires is Mrs. Jane Morbidd, the housekeeper, an American who's worked here nearly 3 years, and whose true background no permanent resident of the castle knows. Mrs. Morbidd was a con artist in New York City, part of a stock swindle gang, until a suspicious customer was killed and she had to flee the country, winding up here, hiding out as the housekeeper and lying low.

Five months ago, someone Mrs. Morbidd knew in the old days showed up at the castle, surprising them both. It was like this: Count Alucard had heard of Dr. Rollo Frankenfield, a skin specialist with a sanitarium on the Riviera, but didn't know Frankenfield was a fraud who flunked out of medical school back in the States. Life as a kind of gigolo and sympathetic companion for elderly rich ladies led Frankenfield to Europe and the founding of the sanitarium. When the count offered a fully equipped lab at the castle, Frankenfield, who had begun to believe in his own researches, said yes.

With Frankenfield came his fiancée, Clara Whiteworthy, who, under her real name of Cora Geckle, used to work in a brothel in New York City, then later plied her trade in Europe as well. She met Frankenfield two years ago, they recognized one another as swindlers, and joined forces.

At the castle, Mrs. Morbidd recognized Cora, though Cora didn't remember Mrs. Morbidd. Not getting any younger, Clara has it in mind to drop Rollo and make a play for the count; the title Countess Alucard, and the money and prestige and safety, matter more to her than skin diseases and age differences. So, when Mrs. Morbidd, needing money to make a better life for herself elsewhere, started blackmail, Clara had no choice but to pay. (She thought of dispatching Mrs. Morbidd to a better world, but Mrs. Morbidd had planned for that eventuality, so Clara was stymied.) Without money of her own, she stole valuable books from the count's library and sold them to an unscrupulous bookdealer during her "shopping" expeditions to Budapest. Clara is unaware that Mrs. Morbidd, keeping an eye on her, knows where the money's coming from.

Meantime, Frankenfield, at the count's request, has been trying unsuccessfully to cure Lily. He thinks Lily's been poisoned somehow, and has a book on poisons from the library in his room to study, but he's getting nowhere. Nor is he accomplishing much in the laboratory, where he spends much of his time, with Eeyore, the lab assistant furnished by Alucard. Eeyore had at one time been a brilliant chemist, but a lab explosion scrambled his brains and he is now a raging lunatic, though harmless.

Hiding in the castle the last two months has been Barry Talmud, an American railway construction engineer, who's just finished a two-year contract working for the Transylvania Transit Authority on the new railway tunnel through Black Mountain. Early in the contract, Barry met a fiery gypsy widow, Madame Openskya. Though opposites in everything, they fell madly in love, married, and lived blissfully together until the contract was finished and Barry ready to return to the States. Madame Openskya had spent 2 years in New York, working in a gypsy tea room. She hated it, insisted Barry stay in Transylvania. When he refused, she started divorce proceedings, and has been trying to serve court papers to hold him in the country. Her relatives watch every road and train. Count Alucard, on the Transit Authority's board of directors, had become friends with Talmud, and offered him a hiding place.

Primeva has been bringing him his meals, but recently, when she had something else to do, she asked Mrs. Morbidd to bring Barry his dinner, unaware that Mrs. Morbidd knew Madame Openskya back in New York. Mrs. Morbidd immediately told Madame Openskya where Barry was, and snuck her into the castle to serve the papers, but Madame Openskya, as we know, got turned around and wound up in the wrong room.

The last two members of our company are Brick and Giddy Newborn, who came to the castle by chance, but are linked with it. Brick is a successful popular novelist, this is his first trip to Europe, and when he said the castle seemed familiar it's because he saw drawings and paintings of these rooms, and the countryside about, in his bride Giddy's house. Giddy, maiden name Strick, is actually the niece of the Alexis Strick murdered by Perffy, which makes Giddy Primeva's first cousin. Giddy's father never got over the disappearance of his sister Alexis, and it was Giddy's idea to take the honeymoon trip here, where Aunt Alexis vanished.

When Joseph Gawker arrived yesterday, he had much more effect on these assembled people than he realized. Giddy Newborn, for instance, had one extracurricular romance before marriage to Brick, who knows nothing about it, and that romance was with Joseph Gawker's brother, Dr. Stephen Gawker. The two brothers look very much alike, which Giddy couldn't help but notice. Nor could Lily Languish; it was Dr. Stephen Gawker whose medical mismanagement had resulted in her parents' deaths. And for Dr. Frankenfield, the big question was whether Joseph Gawker would recognize *him* as a medical school clasmate of Stephen's who'd flunked out and was therefore not a doctor. And Eeyore believed Joseph Gawker *was* his brother Stephen, come to take Eeyore back to the asylum.

Also, Mrs. Morbidd and Clara Whiteworthy both had reason to worry about Gawker's access to the books, because of Clara's thefts to pay blackmail.

Last night, several people were restless and in motion, and saw one another. Both Newborns had trouble sleeping in this strange place and were out of their rooms. Giddy saw the count carrying a tray of food for brother Perffy. Brick and Madame Openskya, who was still looking for Barry, saw one another, recognized one another from having met in New York when Brick was doing research on gypsies for a book, but didn't speak. Coming out of Lily's room with the drug syringe in her hand, Primeva saw Joseph Gawker heading toward the library, and was afraid he'd seen her, but he hadn't. And Eeyore, who likes to look at the pictures in science books in the library, went there last night but didn't go in because Gawker was there. Returning to the lab, he saw Clara Whiteworthy at the other end of the hall— she didn't see him—carrying half a dozen books.

Eeyore was the next to the last person to see Gawker alive. Eeyore would be homicidal if he had the coordination and attention span, but he doesn't; he didn't kill Gawker.

Primeva feared exposure from Gawker, if she'd been spotted with the syringe, but if Primeva were a quick or casual murderer, she would have killed Lily long ago.

Both Barry Talmud and Madmae Openskya are too bound up in their volatile love story to care much about exposure via a third party.

Dr. Frankenfield *did* fear exposure, but it hadn't happened at dinner, and he could hope it never would happen. He decided to just wait and see, and so did Giddy Newborn, who could only hope Stephen Gawker hadn't told his brother about having seduced her.

Mrs. Morbidd, of course, was afraid Gawker would discover Clara Whiteworthy's thefts, which might lead Clara to implicate Mrs. Morbidd, but she too was prepared to wait and see. If worse came to worst, Mrs. Morbidd would take the blackmail money she'd already saved, and skip out.

As for Count Alucard, even if he'd had a motive for doing away with Joseph Gawker, which he had not, he was far too much of a gentleman to murder a guest under his own roof.

Last night, Clara told the count she wanted to make another shopping trip to Budapest. What she intended was to go to the bookdealer, get cheaper editions of books she'd stolen, and replace them before Gawker started his catalog, then re-steal them later. The half dozen stolen books still in her room she took to the library, being seen by Eeyore but not seeing him, and found Gawker already there, in the section she'd been looting.

Only Clara could not afford to wait and see. Only Clara would lose everything—her legitimate reputation, her chance to marry the count—if she didn't act tonight. Getting chloroform from Rollo's lab, she followed Gawker to his room, chloroformed him in his sleep, suffocated him with his pillow, and rubbed crushed garlic on his mouth and the pillow to disguise the smell of chloroform. To confuse diagnosis, she scratched with her hairpin two wounds in the side of his neck to look like Lily's wounds and to feed on the local superstition about vampires. She also opened the window, for the same reason.

Did Clara get away with it? Of course. The local police also believed in vampires, and so never got anywhere, and in fact did not interfere when an enraged crowd attacked the castle and burned it down, with the count, Primeva, Perffy, Lily, Mrs. Morbidd and Eeyore still within.

Clara escaped the inferno, and so did Frankenfield and the Newborns and Barry Talmud and Maria Openskya. The tragedy brought Barry and Maria together again, and they agreed on a compromise; living alternately one year in Transylvania and one in New York. A dozen years later, they went down together on the Titanic, in each other's arms.

Dr. Frankenfield found employment at the local asylum where Dr. Stephen Gawker had once worked, but when his credentials proved fraudulent and he claimed to have discovered lanolin he was transferred from physician to patient, and ended his days there, asking everybody to feel how soft his skin was. A few months after the unsolved murder of Joseph Gawker, police arrested the unscrupulous bookdealer in Budapest for selling pornography to underage nuns. He turned state's evidence, exposed Clara as a book thief, and she was jailed for 6 months, then extradited to America and ended her days in the laundry of a federal prison.

As for the Newborns, they stayed happy and healthy all their lives. Brick Newborn was a famous novelist in his time, though no longer remembered. Melodrama, unfortunately, has just gone out of style.

Answers to the Quiz

Part I

1.k; 2.g; 3.f; 4.c; 5.a; 6.j; 7.d; 8.i; 9.h; 10.e; 11.b

Give yourself five points for each correct answer.

Total: 55

Part II

1.d; 2.a; 3.c; 4.b; 5.b; 6.b&c; 7.c; 8.d; 9.a; 10.c; 11.b; 12.c; 13.d

Give yourself five points for each correct answer.

Total: 65

Part III

1.F; 2.F; 3.T; 4.T; 5.F; 6.T; 7.T; 8.F; 9.F; 10.T

Give yourself five points for each correct answer.

Total: 50

Part IV

1. Clara Whiteworthy killed Joseph Gawker

2. Because she knew he would discover the missing books and inform Count Alucard, who would easily trace her through the rare book dealer in Budapest, thus destroying her dream of becoming Countess Alucard.

Give yourself twenty-five points for each correct answer.

Total: 50

The highest possible score is 220

Anything over 180: Sherlock Holmes

Over 140: Detective First Grade

Over 100: Detective Second Grade

Over 75: Detective Third Grade

Under 75: Inspector Clouzot

If you did poorly (less than 85 points) in the first three sections, but correctly guessed the murderer and the motive, you can congratulate yourself on being an intuitive genius.